We Will Make Waves

A Novel of the White Rose Resistance

Margarita Morris

Landmark Media

Margarita Morris has asserted her right under the Copyright, Designs and Patents Act 1988 to be identified as the author of this work.

margaritamorris.com

Published by Landmark Media, a division of Landmark Internet Ltd.

ISBN: 978-1-0681932-1-7

For Steve

Chapter One

February 1943

I am alone. They have separated me from my brother, Hans, and locked me in a ground-floor room. A table, two chairs. Bare walls. A view out of the back of the building. Bars on the window. It's cold. My fingers are numb.

Hans must be in a similar room. I imagine him pacing the floor, restless. Footsteps echo in the corridor. I stiffen, my pulse quickens. But the guards pass by. I hear voices but not what is said. I sit and wait.

Think Sophie, I tell myself. This is not the first time I've been questioned, but this time is different. I know what to expect. The Gestapo will interrogate us separately, trying to catch us out. They want one of us to crack and tell them the truth. That must never happen. We will never betray our friends. We would rather die than do that.

And to think the day started out so well!

I woke to a bright February morning. A cloudless sky. A smell of spring in the air. The previous evening I had listened to Schubert's *Trout Quintet* on the phonograph and written a letter to my friend Lisa Remppis. I told her how the fourth movement always makes me want to be a trout myself, splashing through the water, full of life and joy.

When I pulled back the curtains this morning, it was as if the promise of the music had been fulfilled. A glorious spring day. Full of hope for the future. I believed that the day would go well. I believed in what we were doing.

I still believe we did the right thing, despite what happened later. That was just bad luck. Or maybe it was my own stupid fault.

We had a suitcase stuffed with anti-Nazi leaflets to take to the university – our goal to lay bare the evil brutality of National Socialism. We want to bring Hitler's regime to an end. We want to stop the war. We call ourselves the White Rose.

Night after night, we've been cranking out leaflets on the mimeograph machine hidden in Eickemeyer's studio. My arm aches from hours turning the handle. But the effort was not in vain. We printed thousands of leaflets ready for distribution. We wanted them to go to people who would understand their significance – university students. People like us.

It was mid-morning when Hans and I left the apartment on Franz-Joseph Strasse. It's only a short walk to the university. Ten minutes, fifteen at the most. Hans carried the suitcase. Not everyone in the White Rose was onboard with the idea of dropping the leaflets at the university. They thought it too risky. So we decided to do it ourselves and not involve anyone else. The plan was to arrive at the university during lectures, deposit the leaflets around the main building, and then leave. Simple.

We headed down Leopoldstrasse which turns into Ludwigstrasse. I love this boulevard with its grand buildings, old churches and triumphal arch topped with four bronze lions. I breathed in the fresh morning air, and felt the sun on my face.

We arrived at the central building of the Ludwig Maximilian University – large, white neo-classical, bordering three sides of a grassy forecourt. Home to the lecture theatres and university administration.

Entering the Lichthof – the glass-domed, galleried atrium at the heart of the building – we ran into our friends Willi Graf and Traute Lafrenz on the grand stone staircase. They are trusted members of the White Rose, but they looked surprised to see us there.

We exchanged greetings.

Willi, ever the thoughtful one, pushed a strand of hair from his forehead, while Traute frowned at the suitcase, eyes sharp with suspicion. She knew. Of course, she knew.

'Where are you two going?' asked Hans. He was relaxed and cheerful. Still, we couldn't afford to waste time chatting.

'The medical clinic,' said Traute. 'Catch up with you both later?'

'Sure. Come round this evening.'

They left and we were alone in the *Lichthof*.

'Ready?' said Hans.

I nodded, keen to get started.

We worked swiftly, silently, placing stacks of leaflets outside lecture halls, on the marble staircase, on windowsills. Wherever people would see them. I returned to the suitcase for more leaflets. Hans grinned at me. It was going well. But we were conscious of the time. Lectures would finish in less than five minutes. We needed to hurry.

'We should go,' said Hans when we'd put leaflets outside every door.

He was right, of course. If we'd gone then, we'd have got out before the lectures ended. No one would have seen us. The source of the leaflets would have remained a mystery.

But there were a few leaflets left. It seemed a shame to waste them. I glanced up at the balcony, then at Hans. He understood immediately.

He grabbed the suitcase and we ran up the stairs, my pulse thrumming with exhilaration. At the top, we stacked the remaining leaflets on the balustrade.

And then I did something stupid.

I don't know what came over me. Maybe it was the bright airiness of the atrium, the adrenaline of the moment. Maybe it was fatigue clouding my judgment. Maybe I just wanted to see the words fly.

With a sweep of my hand, I pushed the leaflets off the balustrade. They fluttered down to the ground like giant snowflakes.

But, unlike snowflakes, they would not melt away.

The words printed on them were too inflammatory. They were intended to set consciences alight.

> *The day of reckoning has come.*
> *Freedom and honour.*
> *Rise up and fight back.*

And then a man walked across the floor of the atrium. We recognised him at once. Jakob Schmidt – university caretaker, Nazi Party member, and part-time Storm Trooper. A real jobsworth and a fanatic to boot. He looked up just as the last few leaflets drifted to the ground. He snatched one up and peered at it. Then his face twisted in rage.

'You two! You're under arrest!'

The lecture hall doors burst open and students flooded out. They swarmed onto the stairs and the landings. They milled about in the atrium. This was our chance. To lose ourselves in the crowd and escape.

We headed for the stairs, diving into the throng, blending with the press of bodies.

But Schmidt was still shouting like a madman. 'Lock the doors! No one leave the building!'

We pressed on. We couldn't afford to stop. We reached the ground floor. The exit was within sight. But the doors were being locked.

'Stop! Criminals!' Schmidt continued to bellow above the chatter.

Panic rippled through the students. The crowd parted. And then Schmidt was there in front of us, breathless, red-faced with triumph.

We stopped running.

'You two are coming with me to the rector's office!' Schmidt licked his lips, no doubt in anticipation of receiving a handsome reward.

We had no choice. We followed him.

I glimpsed Professor Kurt Huber amongst the students. I avoided making eye contact with him or anyone else for that matter. I didn't want to incriminate anyone. But Professor Huber was the author of the words we had just distributed. He'd written a blistering attack on Hitler for all the wasted lives at Stalingrad. And now, he too, could be in danger.

The rector of the university, Dr Walther Wüst, is also a Nazi loyalist. He wouldn't have got the job otherwise. Wüst – mid-forties with neatly trimmed dark hair – listened intently to Schmidt's story – how he had heroically caught us red-handed, throwing subversive leaflets into the atrium. Schmidt gave him a crumpled leaflet as evidence.

Wüst scanned it quickly, his frown deepening. He thanked Schmidt for his diligence and quick-thinking, and then did his duty and phoned the Gestapo.

The Secret Police.

Our family is familiar with the workings of the Gestapo. Hans was once imprisoned for belonging to a banned organisation that promoted hiking and camping, reading books and singing folksongs. As a schoolgirl, I was questioned over Hans's activities, as were my older sister Inge and younger brother Werner. Father has been imprisoned for disparaging remarks about Hitler. The Gestapo thought I was a boy because back then I had short hair. That just shows how dumb they can be. But that doesn't make them any less dangerous.

The Gestapo officer who now arrived in Wüst's office introduced himself as Herr Mohr. He was unremarkable – middle-aged, neat hair, grey suit. He looked like a bank clerk. Mohr and Wüst exchanged the customary 'Heil Hitler' greeting, then Mohr instructed his men to gather all the leaflets from the Lichthof.

Mohr turned to us. 'Identification.'

We handed over our papers. Hans was calm. I tried to be.

'Hans Scholl and Sophie Scholl,' said Mohr, examining our papers, then looking at each of us in turn.

'Yes,' said Hans. I nodded.

Mohr seemed perplexed, as if he couldn't quite believe we were the criminals in question. 'Is that your suitcase?'

'Yes,' said Hans.

'What's in it?'

Hans shrugged. 'Nothing.'

'Open it.'

Hans flipped the latch and lifted the lid. Empty.

Mohr frowned. 'Why are you carrying an empty suitcase?'

'We were going home to Ulm,' said Hans smoothly. 'To collect some fresh laundry.'

Mohr might have believed him, but then his men returned with armfuls of leaflets. Mohr ordered them to put the leaflets into the suitcase. I held my breath and watched.

The leaflets fitted perfectly. Of course they did. The Gestapo had been thorough and had collected every last one.

Mohr's eyes hardened. 'You two have some serious questions to answer.'

While Mohr addressed some matter to Wüst, Hans slid his hand into his trouser pocket. Then he swiftly pulled out a piece of paper, surreptitiously tore it, and stuffed the pieces into his mouth. It was the work of seconds.

The Gestapo were on him in a flash. One held his arms behind his back, another prised his jaw open, and a third retrieved the soggy pieces of paper, dripping with spittle. Mohr ordered them to put the pieces back together on Wüst's desk, ignoring the look of disgust on the rector's face.

'Who wrote this?' roared Mohr, studying the smudged ink which was still mostly legible.

I recognised it as the draft of another leaflet that our friend Christoph Probst had written a few days before. It was the first time he'd written anything for us.

'I don't know,' lied Hans. 'I haven't even read it. A student thrust it into my hands.'

Mohr slammed his fist on the desk. 'Enough. Take them to Wittelsbach Palace.'

My heart missed a beat. The nineteenth-century palace built for the King of Bavaria is now the Gestapo headquarters in Munich. No one enters it willingly. Not everyone leaves.

Handcuffs clicked around our wrists. The officers marched us through the atrium, past the silent crowd. I stared straight ahead. Outside, a black car idled. We were bundled into the back.

And now here we are at Gestapo headquarters, being kept apart so that we can't agree on our story.

My father's favourite quote by Goethe comes to mind. *Allen Gewalten zum trotz, sich erhalten.* Stand tall against all forces, and survive!

May God give me the strength to do just that.

Chapter Two

1936

I was born in May 1921 in the small town of Forchtenberg, nestled in the hills of the Kocher Valley in Württemberg, southwest Germany. Overlooked by the ruins of an old fortification, it was a safe and sheltered place to spend my earliest years. I remember the half-timbered houses with their red-tiled roofs, the banks of the Kocher River, and green wooded hillsides where my siblings, friends, and I would run and play.

I was the fourth of five surviving children. Inge, the eldest, was the sensible big sister we all admired. Then came our brother Hans, sister Elisabeth (Liesl), myself, and finally our brother Werner. We also had a baby sister, Thilde, but she died of pneumonia when she was only one – a dark cloud in an otherwise happy childhood.

At seven, I joined my older siblings in the local primary school. I was a quick learner and soon made my own friends. As a family, we attended services at the Protestant church of St Michael, in the heart of the old town. Music was a shared love, and we sang hymns with enthusiasm.

Looking back, my childhood was idyllic – carefree and full of love. Our parents worked tirelessly to provide a stable home, and I was too young to grasp the political and economic struggles Germany faced after the Great War. That awareness would come later.

Our parents met during the war. My father, Robert Scholl, was a pacifist who enlisted as a medical orderly in 1914 because he refused to fight. My mother, Magdalena Müller, served as a nursing sister in a Lutheran order. They met at a military hospital where both were stationed.

For eleven years, Father served as mayor of Forchtenberg. He was tall, imposing, yet warm and genial, always smartly dressed in a dark suit and tie. He worked hard for the town, though his ambitious plan to connect Forchtenberg to the main railway line met with resistance. In 1930, he lost his re-election bid. We moved south to Ludwigsburg for a couple of years while he worked in Stuttgart. Then in 1932, we moved south again, settling in Ulm, a city on the Danube, where he established himself as a tax and business consultant.

Mother, ten years older than Father, was a quiet, steadying presence. Her deep faith shaped our home, her steadfastness a guiding force. In contrast, Father was outspoken, never afraid to voice his opinions. That trait would eventually land him in trouble.

I was eleven when we arrived in Ulm. City life thrilled us. Our parents rented a large apartment on Münsterplatz, in the shadow of Ulm Minster with its dizzying steeple. Writers and artists frequented our home, filling it with books, music and lively conversation. Yet, we never lost our love for the countryside. We cycled through the hills, explored caves, ran through meadows, and swam in the Iller River. We had the best of both worlds – urban culture and natural beauty.

But the world was changing.

Dark forces were gathering in Germany. Perhaps they had always been there, but I had been too young to notice. Father, however, saw the danger from the start.

I was eleven when Adolf Hitler became Chancellor. The Führer, as he called himself. Father never trusted him. 'That man is the scourge of humanity,' he would say. 'He will destroy this beautiful country of ours.'

But with the self-assurance of youth, we thought we knew better.

Like so many others, my siblings and I were swept up in the fervour of National Socialism. The Weimar Republic, formed after the Great War, had failed, or so Hitler and his followers claimed. The country suffered from unemployment and spiralling inflation. I was just beginning to understand these hardships. Hitler promised to make Germany strong again. The word *Fatherland* evoked images of rolling hills, mountains, rivers, vineyards, forests, and lakes. It meant Goethe and Schiller, Bach and Beethoven. It belonged to all Germans. But postwar defeat and economic ruin had left the nation humiliated. Many were desperate for a leader to restore German pride.

Hitler convinced us – convinced most Germans – that he was that leader.

He spoke of unity. Of prosperity. Every citizen would have bread, freedom, happiness. We would be one *Volk*. And young people were at the heart of his vision. We were the future of the Fatherland.

We couldn't understand why Father opposed Hitler so vehemently. Hans, in particular, often argued with him. Like Father, he was unafraid to speak his mind.

'Hasn't the Führer kept his promise to eliminate unemployment?' Hans asked one evening at dinner. 'Look at the mess after the war – inflation, joblessness. Now the economy is growing. Germany is finding its strength again.' He had likely heard this at school, or on the radio, or read it in a newspaper. He could have been a Party spokesman.

We waited for Father's response.

He speared a potato with his fork as if stabbing Hitler himself. 'Have you stopped to consider *why* unemployment is falling? That man is cranking up the war industry. He's building barracks. He's re-arming Germany. Where do you think that will lead?' He waited for an answer, enjoying the debate.

'Hitler is also building motorways,' Werner added.

'So he can roll his tanks down them!' Father shot back. 'You'll see.'

'There's no evidence that's why he's building them,' said Inge. 'They'll allow ordinary people to travel more easily.'

Father leaned forward. 'When times are hard, people believe promises without asking, *Who is making them?*'

The argument rolled on, as they always did in those days. Our family debated National Socialism constantly. We had been raised to speak freely, without fear of judgement. But tensions were rising.

Mother, ever the peacemaker, interjected. 'More potatoes anyone?'

'Yes, please.' I took some and passed the dish to Liesl.

Personally, I had no issue with the motorways – so long as Hitler didn't carve them through my beloved mountains or disrupt the lakes and rivers where I loved to swim. I didn't want cars and lorries disturbing the birdsong. I said as much.

Father chuckled and patted my hand. 'Wise words, Sophie.'

Mother shot me a grateful smile.

For now, the tension eased. The conversation drifted to other topics.

But it was only a matter of time before the next argument erupted.

'The Nazis are all wolves! Can't you see how they are manipulating the German people? What they are doing is shameful!' Father's voice rose, his frustration spilling into the hallway. He was trying to make Hans see reason, but Hans wasn't listening. None of us really listened when Father started on about Hitler, the Party, and the so-called evils of National Socialism.

'You don't understand,' said Hans, adjusting his black neckerchief in the hallway mirror and smoothing his hair with his palm. He cut a dashing figure in his Hitler Youth uniform. 'Haven't you heard that the former British Prime Minister Lloyd George thinks that Hitler is a great leader?'

'I think I understand Hitler better than Lloyd George does! What does he know about Germany?'

'I'm going to a meeting,' Hans said curtly, slamming the front door behind him.

Father sighed and retreated to his study. He hated that we had all joined the Hitler Youth, but he was a liberal at heart. He believed in free choice, even when that meant allowing us to make what he saw as the wrong decisions. It must have been a terribly difficult time for him.

Hans, never one to do things by halves, threw himself into the Hitler Youth with fervour. He wanted to make a difference, and I admired his determination. The Youth leaders even presented him with a dagger inscribed with *Blood and Honour*. How romantic that seemed! We all admired Hans's dagger, though Mother worried it was too sharp. Werner soon followed him into the Hitler Youth through the ranks of the *Jungvolk*.

Inge and Liesl were in the League of German Girls so, naturally, I joined too, along with my school friends, Annelies Kammerer and Susanne Hirzel. Likewise, my friend Lisa Remppis who lived in Leonberg near Stuttgart. I had got to know her through visits to our aunt who lived in the same building.

The only friend who wasn't allowed to join was Luise Nathan because she was Jewish. The rule struck me as ridiculous, and I told her so.

'With your blonde hair and blue eyes, you look more Aryan than I do,' I said. My own hair was dark brown, my eyes the same.

Luise shrugged. 'I don't want to be where I'm not welcome.' She tried to sound indifferent, but it was clear the exclusion hurt. Still, it didn't stop me from signing up. I was a child, and children can be thoughtless.

I wore my uniform with pride. Navy-blue skirt, open-necked white blouse, loose black tie, white ankle socks.

What is it about a uniform that makes it so appealing, especially to the young? I suppose it offers a sense of belonging, proof that you are part of something greater. It breaks down barriers between strangers, making friendship easier. You feel accepted. And isn't that what every young person wants? It's much easier than standing alone.

And what a time we had! In my memory, we were always singing – hearty songs with rousing tunes and foot-tapping rhythms, dedicating ourselves to the Fatherland. We engaged in sport – swimming, gymnastics, running – becoming strong and fit. Swimming has always been a passion of mine and I relished every opportunity. But best of all were the hikes through the Swabian Jura, cooking over campfires, singing under the stars.

Inge quickly rose through the ranks. She had a natural command, being the eldest, and could be quite bossy. It suited her well. Soon, she was promoted to *Ringführerin*, or Circle Leader, leading a group of younger girls. Liesl joined her and together they ran their Circle with enthusiasm. Many of our activities – hiking, camping, folk singing –

stemmed from older Youth Movement traditions that had existed long before the Nazis. The only difference was the ideology woven into our activities.

Susanne and I were only fourteen when we were each put in charge of a dozen younger girls. At fourteen you are still so young, but you believe yourself terribly grown-up.

On Thursday evenings, Inge led educational meetings for leaders which Susanne and I attended. The younger girls practically worshipped her. She guided us through discussions on Nazi ideology – the importance of racial purity, the sacred duty of motherhood, and, above all, unwavering loyalty to the Führer. We learned household skills: cooking, sewing, childcare. Hitler once said he had a horror of women meddling in politics. The Nazi motto for women was *Kinder, Küche, Kirche*. Children, kitchen, church. That was the world we were expected to inhabit. But we were young, and motherhood felt a lifetime away.

What did I make of all this propaganda? Looking back, it's difficult to understand why I wasn't more critical. But then, no one was. Hitler knew exactly what he was doing by focusing on young people. We were malleable, easy to shape. And children can be the harshest enforcers of rules, for they lack empathy, have no patience for dissent. The system thrived by putting older children in charge of younger ones. It ensured discipline. It ensured obedience.

In 1936, at fifteen, I was promoted to *Führerin*, leading a platoon of fifty girls. A year later, I became *Gruppenführerin*. Inge and Elisabeth, both ardent members of the League, set the example, and I followed. Once, when a girl failed to attend one of my Saturday meetings because she was helping in her family's butcher's shop, I sent the police to fetch her. I made my girls pool their food into a communal stash and then grab for it blindfold, believing this would teach fairness. Some parents criticised me for what they saw as 'communist' behaviour, but I was in charge and these were my rules. When we went camping, I forced my girls to stay up all night singing around the campfire instead of letting them sleep in their warm sleeping bags. I believed we should be as tough as the boys in the Hitler Youth, that we should meet their standards.

At the time, I thought I was leading. I thought I was shaping something strong. I didn't realise how much we were being shaped ourselves.

In the summer of 1936 – the summer that Berlin hosted the Olympic Games – I was fifteen and Hans was seventeen, soon to be eighteen. I suppose you could say I was something of a tomboy. I wore my hair short, in a boyish cut, and loved physical activity – swimming, climbing trees, running through fields. I wasn't like Inge, clever and responsible, nor was I demure and feminine like Liesl. I played the flute and the piano and I enjoyed drawing, but otherwise I didn't conform to people's expectations of a young woman. I had a habit of speaking my mind, and that didn't always go down well.

Hans, on the other hand, was the ideal young man – bright, charming, and handsome. Tall and lean, with thick, wavy dark hair and an engaging smile, he commanded attention. The girls in my class thought him very good-looking, and I'm sure more than a few were secretly in love with him. He had risen quickly through the ranks of the Hitler Youth, becoming a squad leader in charge of one hundred and fifty boys. That alone was impressive, but when he was chosen to carry his squad's banner at the Nuremberg Party Rally in September, we were ecstatic. He was going to see and hear the Führer in person. How I envied him.

Father, of course, was not pleased. But that was to be expected. Mother focused on practical matters, ensuring Hans had everything he needed for the week-long trip. They would be camping in endless rows of white tents in a vast field. I thought it sounded terribly romantic.

Inge and I saw him off at Ulm train station. What a sight it was – crowds of Hitler Youth, the future of Germany, standing proudly in their freshly laundered, meticulously pressed uniforms. The train, specially chartered for the journey to Nuremberg, was decorated with bunting, adding to the celebratory atmosphere. The station was filled with an air of anticipation, of excitement. We waved Hans off and wished him good luck, imagining him marching through Nuremberg's medieval streets, past half-timbered houses and cheering crowds.

Nuremberg was a city steeped in history and culture, home to Albrecht Dürer, the great Renaissance artist, and the Meistersinger, the medieval craftsmen who were also poets and musicians. But it was also the city of the future – the Nazis had built a vast new stadium to house their rallies. The new Germany, they claimed, would stand upon the foundations of the old, merging past and future to create something glorious. This was how the Fatherland would be great again.

With Hans away, the apartment in Ulm felt strangely quiet. There were no heated debates over Hitler's motorways, no laughter, no teasing. I missed him. I went about my days as usual, attending school, spending time with my friends, but my thoughts kept drifting to him. Had he seen the Führer yet? What was it like? I longed for his return, eager to hear every detail – the rally, the parades, the military displays, and, above all, the speeches. Listening on the radio wasn't the same.

We wanted to hear it from someone who had been there, who had seen it firsthand.

But when Hans returned, he was different. Something had changed.

The moment I heard his footsteps in the hallway, I dropped my book and rushed to meet him.

'Well?' I asked eagerly. 'How was it?'

'Oh, you know.' He shrugged, dropping his rucksack onto the floor. He looked tired, withdrawn.

'Give him a chance to settle in,' Mother said, coming in from the kitchen. 'He's only just walked through the door. You must be hungry,' she added, addressing Hans.

'I'll go and get changed,' he muttered, loosening his necktie before disappearing into the room he shared with Werner, shutting the door behind him.

'What's wrong with him?' I asked, frowning.

'He's probably just exhausted,' Mother said. 'All that marching and excitement – it must have been overwhelming.'

She was trying to reassure me, but the crease in her forehead betrayed her concern.

At dinner, Hans barely ate. He pushed his food around his plate before excusing himself early. That wasn't like him at all. I exchanged a glance with Inge, but she looked just as perplexed as I was.

Days passed, and Hans remained distant. He avoided conversation, refused to talk about the rally. If it was just exhaustion, he should have recovered by now. The other girls at school gushed about what their brothers had seen in Nuremberg – the grandeur, the speeches, the spectacle. But from Hans, we heard nothing. Inge prodded him with gentle questions. Had he seen the Führer? What was the parade ground like? But he kept his thoughts locked away. I grew frustrated.

Then, one evening after dinner, Inge suggested a walk along the Danube. I immediately agreed – I knew what she was up to. Hans hesitated, but between us, we managed to persuade him.

We set off from Münsterplatz, strolling past the town hall with its colourful frescoes, past the medieval Metzger Tower, leaning – not as dramatically as the tower of Pisa, but enough to be noticeable. Then, under the old city wall, we took the footpath along the river. It was a warm autumn evening, perfect for a quiet conversation.

Hans was looking more like himself. Something in the fresh air, in the quiet of the river, seemed to settle him.

'The weather was perfect,' he said finally. 'Not a cloud in the sky. *Hitler Weather,* they call it. As if the Führer controls the heavens.' He let out a short, humourless laugh. 'Ridiculous, don't you think?'

It was the first time I had ever heard him say anything remotely critical of Hitler. I held my tongue, afraid to say the wrong thing, afraid he might close up again.

'What was the rally like?' asked Inge gently.

'Oh, it was spectacular,' Hans admitted. 'We marched through the old town, lined up in perfect formation, thousands of us. The streets were packed with cheering crowds. It was... electrifying.'

He hesitated, then continued.

'But then something strange happened. It's hard to explain. The drumbeats, the marching... it was hypnotic. And suddenly, I felt like I was on autopilot. I had this... out-of-body experience. As if I were watching from above. And I thought – *we're just ants. Thousands of ants, following without thinking.* And then it hit me – *who am I?* And the answer was... *nobody.* I was completely insignificant.'

'So what did you do?' Inge asked.

'Nothing,' Hans said. 'I couldn't do anything. I was carrying our squad's banner. I was supposed to feel proud. Instead I felt...' He paused, searching for the word. 'Dehumanised.'

We walked in silence, absorbing his words.

'And the parade ground?' I asked.

'It's called the Zeppelin Field,' Hans said. 'Count Zeppelin's airships landed there in 1909. And now, Albert Speer, Hitler's architect, has designed this enormous grandstand with tiers of limestone seating and columns, like the biggest Greek temple ever. Hitler and other Party top dogs stand on a big platform beneath a carved Swastika. When the sun hits the limestone, it glows bright white.'

It sounded mythological. Hans continued.

'There were a hundred thousand people in the stands, music blaring – *Horst Wessel Lied, Deutschland über alles*. We marched and sang, like robots, shouting *Heil Hitler! Sieg Heil!* There was no need to think. And then fighter planes roared overhead. Tanks rolled past. It was deafening. And all I could think was – *Father was right.* Hitler is cranking up the war machine. And it terrified me.'

A shiver ran down my spine.

'And Hitler?' I asked. 'Did you see him?'

'Yes. He spoke about how we were Germany's future, how we had to raise the flag from the chaos.' Hans shook his head. 'And I kept thinking – *what chaos? Who is creating this chaos?* I tried to discuss what we'd heard with some of the older boys, but it was hopeless. No one wanted to think for themselves. It was impossible to have an intelligent conversation.'

We walked on. The first crack in our faith had appeared. And nothing would ever be the same again.

Chapter Three

February 1943

H err Mohr sits in his large chair behind an even larger desk. I sit opposite him on a hard, wooden chair, its straight back offering no comfort. In the corner, a female stenographer shuffles papers, avoiding my eye. She keeps her head down, pretending to be invisible.

I turn my attention back to Mohr, trying to read what sort of man he is. His face reveals nothing. His dark hair, slicked back, mirrors the style of Dr Wüst. He is probably in his forties, a man who could easily pass for a bank manager or a bureaucrat in any government office. Grey, neat, unremarkable. But he is Gestapo, and that makes him dangerous. He is my enemy. I must never forget that.

To begin with, there is the tedious ritual of form-filling.

Full name: Sophia Magdalena Scholl – though everyone calls me Sophie. Occupation: student. Income: 150 Marks per month from my parents. Date and place of birth: May 9, 1921, Forchtenberg, Württemberg. Current address in Munich: 23 Franz-Joseph Strasse 13, Ground Floor, Garden House c/o Schmidt. Not the same Schmidt as the caretaker who arrested us, of course. Schmidt is a very common name in Germany. Our landlady, Frau Schmidt, spends most of her time in the countryside, frightened out of the city by the bombing raids.

More questions.

Citizenship: German Reich. Religion: Lutheran. Are my parents and grandparents of German blood? Yes. Marital status? Single – after all, I am only twenty-one.

Mohr continues, his tone detached, asking about my parents' names and occupations, my passport, my driving licence. Even a hunting licence, of all things. What would I do with a hunting licence? The irony is not lost on me – Father once threatened that if anything happened to us, he would shoot Hitler himself. Perhaps a hunting licence would have come in handy after all.

I was once a member of the League of German Girls, so that goes on the form. I provide details of my time in the Reich Labour Service, an experience I recall as one of the most miserable of my life.

On paper, I am the perfect German citizen. My ancestry is unblemished. My bloodline, pure. True, my shoulder-length hair is dark rather than the preferred Aryan blonde, but I'm neither Jewish nor Communist. Not that it should matter. But at least Mohr cannot use that against me.

Still, he must be wondering why I am here, sitting in his office, taking up his valuable time.

He lights a cigarette and offers me one. I shake my head. 'No thank you.'

'You don't smoke?'

'Only occasionally.'

He takes a slow drag, blowing the smoke toward the ceiling. 'You admit, Fräulein Scholl, that you pushed a pile of leaflets off the balcony of the Lichthof this morning?'

Outside, the sun is shining. I long to feel it on my face. My best chance of getting out of here is to admit what cannot be denied.

'Pushing the leaflets off the balcony was a stupid prank,' I say. 'One that I now regret. I would like to apologise for my childish behaviour.' I mean every word and hope my sincerity will be enough to soften him. Of course, it isn't.

'Did you put the leaflets there in the first place?'

'I don't know where they came from.'

Mohr looks unconvinced. He circles back to the same questions he asked at the university, hoping I will contradict myself. I don't.

I repeat exactly what we said in Rector Wüst's office. We were on our way to Ulm. The empty suitcase was to bring back fresh laundry. We know nothing about the leaflets.

'You didn't have any dirty laundry to take back to Ulm?'

'No, I wash small things by hand.'

'If you were going to Ulm, why stop at the university at all?'

A good question. Fortunately, I have an answer.

'Yesterday, I met my friend Gisela Schertling in the English Gardens for supper. We arranged for her to come to the apartment at noon today for lunch. But last night, talking to Hans, we decided to travel to Ulm instead. It was a last-minute decision. It would allow us to see a family friend before she returned to Hamburg and also collect fresh laundry. I needed to let Gisela know about the change of plan, so I asked Hans if we could stop by the university on our way to the train station. I knew she would be at Dr. Huber's *Introduction to Philosophy* lecture, which was due to end at eleven. We arrived ten minutes early.'

Most of what I have said can be verified – the plan to meet Gisela for lunch, her attendance at the lecture. Only the part about informing her of our change of plans is untrue. Mohr seems vaguely convinced, but not enough to let me go.

'When my men collected the leaflets this morning, they fitted exactly into your empty suitcase. How do you explain that?'

'A coincidence.'

'I doubt that very much. Did you see anyone when you arrived at the university?'

'Yes. Our friends Willi Graf and Traute Lafrenz.'

'Did you speak to them?'

'Just to say hello. They were on their way to the medical clinic.'

'What did you do then?'

'Dr Huber's lecture wasn't finished so I couldn't see Gisela immediately. I took Hans upstairs to show him the Psychological Institute where I often attend lectures. It's on the third floor.' My mind races ahead as I invent my story. The words spill from my lips. 'When we reached the top floor, we found a stack of leaflets on the marble balustrade. We had already seen others scattered around the building. We each picked one up, glanced at it, and put it back.' There's no point denying we saw the leaflets. They were clearly visible – we'd made sure of that! 'I couldn't resist pushing the pile off the balustrade,' I add. 'It was a silly impulse, something I now regret. If I could go back in time, I wouldn't do it again.'

Mohr watches me, trying to work out if I'm lying. I hold my ground. Somewhere, Hans is being asked the same questions, giving the same answers. Thinking of my brother gives me the strength I need.

Mohr is the first to look away. He frowns at his notes, his fingers tapping the desk. Is he unsettled? Perhaps. He has likely spent months tracking down the authors of these leaflets, expecting hardened radicals – people he could easily loathe. Instead, he finds two respectable students from a middle-class family in Ulm.

Does he have children of his own? The thought crosses my mind.

Then his expression darkens. He slams his hand onto the pile of leaflets. 'These are treason!'

I do not argue. It would be foolish.

'Anyone found guilty of high treason faces the death sentence!'

I already know this. His threats only solidify my determination.

'Who wrote and printed these leaflets?'

'I don't know.'

He reaches into a drawer and pulls out another leaflet. I recognise it immediately. 'This one is headed *A Call to All Germans*. This and others like it have appeared in Stuttgart, Vienna, Ulm, Frankfurt, Hamburg, Augsburg.' He reels them off on his fingers. 'They were not all posted from here in Munich.'

I feign surprise. Of course, I know they weren't. I posted them myself in Augsburg. I sense his frustration. The Gestapo are stumped. They don't know if they're dealing with a handful of dissidents in Munich or a nationwide resistance movement threatening to topple the Nazi state.

Mohr exhales sharply. 'Fräulein Scholl, you are currently looking very suspicious. I advise you to tell the truth.'

I meet his gaze, steady. 'It was foolish of me to push the leaflets off the balcony,' I repeat. 'But beyond that, I know nothing.'

Chapter Four

1937

Hans's disillusionment at Nuremberg did little to dampen my own enthusiasm for the League of German Girls. I wore my hair short, in a boyish cut, and led my group with strict discipline. As a group leader, I organised hikes and camping trips, where we sang, laughed, and talked late into the night around the fire. The camaraderie was real, the friendships genuine. Yet beneath the surface, I was beginning to see cracks in the foundation of National Socialism. But we tried not to let that spoil our fun – we were just teenage girls, enjoying ourselves.

Despite his misgivings, Hans continued his role in the Hitler Youth out of loyalty to his squad. He wasn't about to abandon them simply because the Party Rally had left him uneasy.

But the doubts were growing. We had been raised to think for ourselves, to question, to debate. Father had encouraged it, and our dinner table had always been a place of lively discussion. Yet National Socialism and independent thinking were at odds. The leaders of the Hitler Youth tolerated no questions, no challenges to doctrine. And soon, Hans learned that firsthand.

One afternoon, during a break between drills, he sat down to read a book – *The Tide of Fortune* by Stefan Zweig, one of his favourite authors. The essays chronicle turning points in history – the discovery of the Pacific Ocean, the conquest of the South Pole, Waterloo, Goethe, Dostoyevsky. Zweig has an extraordinary ability to capture the human condition in elegant prose. He is worth reading.

Hans had barely turned a page when a shadow fell over him, blocking the light.

'What's this?' The book was snatched from his hands.

'Hey!' Hans jumped to his feet. 'Give that back.'

The culprit was Kurt, the leader of Hans's Hitler Youth company. A thug who relished throwing his weight around.

Hans squared his shoulders. 'It's a collection of essays by Stefan Zweig.' He resisted the urge to add, *A famous Austrian writer, if you've never heard of him.* Provoking Kurt wouldn't help.

Kurt's lip curled. 'Don't you know this filth is forbidden? The author is a Jew!'

Hans clenched his fists. We knew many Jews in Ulm – Father's colleagues, family friends.

'What does his religion have to do with anything?' Hans snapped. 'He writes about history. About people who shaped the world.'

'There is only one person whose words you need to read and follow.'

'If you mean Hitler—'

'Of course I mean the Führer! Who else?'

Hans bit his tongue, resisting the urge to say that *Mein Kampf* was written in such dreadful prose that he'd rather pull his own teeth out than read it. Zweig, on the other hand, was a master of language. But there was no point arguing.

'May I have my book back if I promise not to read it here?' he asked coolly.

Kurt tossed it at him and stalked off. Hans shoved the book into his rucksack, relieved to have got away with it. But the encounter left a bitter taste.

Not long after, I had a similar experience.

An important League of German Girls leader visited Ulm for an evening of ideological training. It was not as enjoyable as our outdoor activities, but deemed essential to our education. The leader, Fräulein Koch, stood before us and asked for book recommendations.

I raised my hand. 'Heinrich Heine,' I said confidently. I loved his poetry – clever, full of wit and gentle irony, never heavy or dull.

Fräulein Koch inhaled sharply. Her eyes widened in horror.

'What is your name, girl?'

'Sophie Scholl.' A ripple of silence spread through the room. I held my gaze steady.

'Well, Sophie Scholl, your suggestion reveals that you still have degenerate Jewish writings in your home.' She practically spat out the words. 'Are you not aware that such works were banned by Propaganda Minister Goebbels in 1933?'

I faltered. Of course we had Heine's books at home. Didn't everyone? We read all the great German writers – Goethe, Schiller, Heine, Kafka, Thomas Mann, Stefan Zweig.

'Well?' Fräulein Koch demanded.

Anger flared in my chest. I despised the way she spoke to me as if I were ignorant, when in reality, she was the one who lacked understanding. The words burst from me before I could stop them. 'Whoever does not know Heine does not know German literature.'

Her nostrils flared. 'Enough, girl!'

I clenched my jaw.

'You would be wise to keep quiet.'

So I did. For the rest of the evening, I said nothing at all.

I put the Heine incident behind me and continued to enjoy outdoor activities with the League of German Girls. One cycling trip stands out in my memory. We followed the winding paths of rivers, weaving through lush green valleys crowned with ancient hilltop castles. We rode through sleepy villages, the sun warming our faces, a gentle breeze keeping us cool. This was the Germany I loved – the beauty of its landscapes, the richness of its history. In those moments, it felt as if all was right with the world.

We set up camp in a field beside a stream. I shared a tent with my sister, Inge.

In the evening, we gathered wood, built a campfire, and cooked sausages on sticks. The fire attracted insects, which the other girls swatted away in irritation, but I watched them with fascination. To me, they were a sign of the abundance of God's creation. Insect life seemed far more harmonious than human life.

After we had eaten, we lay back on the grass and gazed up at the darkening sky. One by one, the stars emerged, tiny pinpricks of light like scattered diamonds. It was the perfect end to a perfect day.

Our conversation drifted from one topic to another. Then, out of nowhere, one of the girls, Ingrid, said, 'You know, everything would be just wonderful if it weren't for this dreadful business with the Jews. That's what I can't handle.'

A chill seemed to sweep through the camp. A shiver ran down my spine. Ingrid had dared to voice something that had been troubling me ever since my friend Luise had been barred from joining the League of German Girls. Why did Hitler hate the Jews so much?

The troop leader responded with some vague rhetoric about trusting the Führer to know what was best for Germany. She insisted that we had to accept difficult things for the greater good, even if we didn't fully understand them.

I doubted Ingrid was convinced. I certainly wasn't.

The conversation soon moved on to lighter topics, though I barely registered what was said. The moment had passed, but something had changed. The mood was subdued. We were all tired after the long ride, and before long, we climbed into our tents.

The next morning, the sun was shining, and we had another day of cycling ahead of us. Everyone behaved as if the awkward exchange of the previous evening had never happened. But a seed of doubt had been planted in my mind. It would take root, grow, and start to strangle my faith in National Socialism.

One by one, each of us Scholl children began to see the realities of the regime for ourselves. And we didn't like what we saw.

For Hans, the final straw came when his squad dared to be different. He had the idea that his boys should design and make their own flag – a symbol of their unity as a group. The boys were eager. The first task was deciding what to put on it.

After much discussion, they settled on a griffin – a mythical beast with the body of a lion and the head and wings of an eagle. It was a fitting choice, combining the king of the beasts with the king of the skies, a symbol of power and majesty. But most importantly, it was *their* flag.

It was a true collaborative effort. The boys brought in scraps of fabric salvaged from their mothers' sewing boxes, along with needles, thread, and scissors. Hans sketched a griffin onto a large sheet of paper, copying it from a book. They cut out the design and pinned it to a piece of gold cloth. When the sewing was done, the flag was magnificent, even if some of the stitches were uneven. That didn't matter. It was their creation – far more distinctive than the standard swastika banners. They mounted it proudly on a wooden pole.

Then they held a dedication ceremony.

'We hereby dedicate this flag to the Führer, the leader of our great country. We promise to be loyal to it at all times.'

A few days later, Hans and his squad lined up on the parade ground with the other groups. A senior Hitler Youth leader was present to inspect them. Hans's squad stood proudly, their griffin flag snapping in the breeze. Hans had given the honour of carrying it to Dieter, the twelve-year-old boy who had first suggested the griffin as their emblem.

As the visiting leader strode up and down the ranks, his sharp gaze took in the squads. All bore the prescribed swastika flags – except Hans's group.

He came to a sudden halt. His eyes narrowed. 'What is *that*?' he demanded, glaring at the banner. He frowned as if he had never seen such a thing before. Hans didn't like his tone.

'It's our troop banner,' he said. 'We made it ourselves.'

'Hand it over. *Now.*'

Dieter flinched but tightened his grip on the pole.

'I *said* hand it over!' The leader's voice rose to a shout. 'You are not permitted to fly your own flag. The only acceptable flags are those approved in the manuals.'

Hans stood firm. 'We dedicated this flag to the Führer. It's a symbol of our loyalty as a group.'

But the leader wasn't listening. Without warning, he lunged for the pole, trying to tear it from Dieter's grasp. The boy held on desperately.

Hans had had enough.

He stepped forward, putting himself between Dieter and the leader. 'Let him keep the flag. What harm does it do? Stop being such a bully!'

The leader's face darkened with fury. He shoved past Hans, reaching again for the flag. That was when Hans snapped. Without thinking, his fist clenched, and he threw a punch, landing it squarely on the leader's ear.

The man staggered back, his hand flying to his ear, his expression shifting from shock to blind rage. Around them, the boys gasped. The silence that followed was deafening.

The leader recovered quickly, stepping forward until he was inches from Hans's face. He jabbed a finger into his chest, spitting with rage. 'You are *demoted!*'

Hans shrugged. 'Fine,' he said flatly. He no longer cared.

It wasn't in Hans's nature to stay downcast for long, and after he was demoted from the Hitler Youth, he soon found a group far better suited to his way of thinking. The dj.1.11. was so named because it had been founded on 1 November 1929. Although the Nazis had banned it in 1933, it still thrived underground. I suspect the clandestine nature of the organisation appealed to Hans as much as anything. Werner joined him, and together they embarked on a series of adventures. If the group had been open to girls, I would have joined too!

Hans was far happier in his new surroundings, making friends who shared his outlook on life. He had grown tired of the monotonous marching and endless saluting that defined the Hitler Youth. There was none of that in the dj.1.11. The worst thing about the Hitler

Youth, for Hans, had been the restrictions on his intellectual freedom. But this group was all about freedom and individuality. They played sport, went hiking, camped in black *kohte* tents like wigwams, debated philosophy, and sang Cossack folksongs, Balkan ballads – even American cowboy songs that would have been strictly forbidden by the Hitler Youth leaders. Some of their behaviour was downright reckless. They delighted in telling jokes that, if overheard, could have got them arrested.

'Hey, Sophie,' Hans said one day, eyes twinkling mischievously. 'What is an Aryan?'

I recognised that teasing look. 'What?' I asked.

'Someone as blond as Hitler, as tall as Goebbels, and as slim as Göring.'

I laughed. This group suited him far better than the Hitler Youth ever had.

When he wasn't out with his new friends, Hans scribbled in his notebooks – song lyrics, poems, thoughts, observations. Anything and everything. Those notebooks would one day put us all at risk, though in 1937, we didn't yet grasp the danger.

Hans was soon to graduate from secondary school. He intended to study medicine at university, but those plans would have to wait. First, he was required to spend six months at a camp in Göppingen, working for the Reich Labour Service. He would be helping to build Hitler's new Autobahns – the very motorways that, according to Father, were destined to carry tanks. He would have to wear a uniform and be bossed around by the same type of men he had encountered in the Hitler Youth. He wasn't looking forward to it.

Meanwhile, I remained in the League of German Girls, but the endless rules and absurdities were beginning to grate on me. More and more, I sought solace in my art. I have always loved to draw, and one of my favourite pastimes was curling up on the sofa with my sketchpad and pencils, losing myself in my sketches. I drew family members, the children of friends and neighbours, animals – whoever or whatever caught my eye. I illustrated stories, bringing words to life. I don't mean to boast, but everyone said I was very good.

People assumed I would study art after leaving school. But I've never believed that art is something that can truly be taught. Of course, one can learn the technical aspects – perspective, anatomy, composition. Hand-eye coordination improves with practice, much like playing the piano. But that isn't what it means to be an artist. A real artist has to have something to *say*, and for that, one first has to become a person of experience. That isn't something anyone can teach in a classroom. And besides, who was I to think I would ever have anything interesting to say? I was a nobody.

Yet drawing gave me peace of mind, a deep satisfaction when a sketch took on a life of its own. Looking back, I wonder if I was subconsciously trying to escape the world around me – a world that was becoming ever more oppressive and frightening.

Take, for example, what happened to one of the teachers at our school in Ulm. A popular, well-respected man. One day, he simply disappeared. No explanation. No warning.

Rumours spread. We heard that he had been forced to stand in front of a squad of Storm Troopers – the Nazi paramilitary, known as the Brownshirts because of their uniforms – while they spat in his face. Then he had vanished, sent to a camp. We heard someone mention *Dachau*.

When Hans and Inge asked his mother what he had done, her answer chilled us to the bone.

'Nothing. He did *nothing*. He just wasn't a Nazi like them.'

We turned to Father. 'What is a concentration camp?'

His face darkened. 'It is war,' he said grimly. 'That man is waging war against his own people. A war against defenceless individuals. A war against our freedoms.'

We were stunned. How could such things be happening in our beloved Fatherland? We weren't at war with anyone. It made no sense.

'But, Father,' we protested, 'doesn't the Führer know about these camps? If he did, surely he would stop it?'

Father's expression grew thunderous. 'Of course he knows!' he raged. 'How could he *not*? They have existed for years, built by his closest supporters. And he does *nothing* to stop them. Those who survive are forbidden to speak of what they endured. On pain of death.'

On pain of death.

We never saw the teacher again.

Chapter Five

February 1943

A fter hours of relentless questioning, during which I continue to deny all knowledge of the leaflets, Mohr finally decides he has had enough – for now. I suspect he wants to go home. So do I, but I won't be sleeping in my own bed tonight.

Mohr hands me over to his subordinate, Herr Lohner. Lohner escorts me to a woman who records my details and instructs me to surrender my watch and jewellery. She is brisk and efficient. The guards stand close, watching our every move.

'Come this way.' She leads me into another room and closes the door behind us.

The moment we are alone, her manner changes completely. She looks directly at me and smiles.

'Hello, Sophie.'

I hesitate. 'Hello.'

I am not sure what to make of her. She is not the type of person I expected to find in a place like this, working for the Gestapo. She wears no uniform, just a plain skirt and blouse. Her fine auburn hair is swept into a bun, though a few loose strands have escaped. She looks to be in her mid-thirties.

'I need you to undress,' she says, her voice gentle, almost apologetic. 'I have to conduct a full search. It's the rules.'

My suspicion flares. Has she been planted here to trick me into confessing something?

'Hurry,' she whispers. 'Or the guards will come in.'

I pull off my cardigan, unbutton my blouse, and slip it off. I step out of my skirt and stand in my underwear. The room is cold, and I shiver.

'That will do,' she says. Then she moves closer, lowering her voice to a whisper. 'My name is Else Gebel. I'm a political prisoner, like you. Quick, if you have anything incriminating, give it to me. I will destroy it.'

I blink in surprise. If I were carrying something, would she really help me? Or would she take it straight to Mohr as evidence? I search her face for any sign of deceit.

'You have to trust me, Sophie. Please.'

I look into her eyes and see nothing but sincerity and understanding.

'I have nothing,' I say. It's the truth. I'm not carrying any leaflets or drafts like the one Hans had in his pocket.

Else exhales in relief. 'That's good. Get dressed.'

I pull my clothes back on quickly, grateful I am at least allowed to keep them. Else opens the door and resumes her detached, businesslike demeanour in front of the guards.

A guard leads us down a series of dreary corridors and unlocks a heavy metal door. Inside is a small, bare cell with plain plastered walls, a hard floor, two narrow single beds, a wooden table and chairs, and a toilet in the corner.

I hesitate, but Else gives me a small nod, and I step inside. The guard locks the door behind us.

'I hope you don't mind sharing with me,' she says.

'So you can keep an eye on me?'

'Something like that.'

'Don't worry, I'm not going to do anything reckless.'

'I'm glad to hear it.'

'I don't mind sharing,' I add. 'I grew up in a large family – I'm used to it.'

Else steps closer, lowering her voice. 'Listen to me, Sophie. A word of advice. Say nothing they can't prove.'

'That's exactly what I'm doing.'

'Good.'

She has shown me kindness, and I want to offer something in return. I don't know how long she has been here, but I doubt she gets much news from the outside world. So I give her the only thing I have – hope.

'You know, the war is going badly for Germany,' I say. 'It won't be long before the Allies invade, and then this barbarism will end. Hitler will be defeated. It's only a matter of time.'

She smiles and takes my hand. 'I hope you're right, Sophie.'

I smile back. I know we are going to be friends.

Chapter Six

1937

In May 1937, I turned sixteen. My growing awareness of the evils of National Socialism coloured my attitude towards life, particularly school, where I started to feel like an outsider. I had once loved school, but now it became odious to me, warped by the distorting prism of Nazi ideology.

In history, for example, we were taught that the Aryan race was superior to all others. The Treaty of Versailles, which had shaped post-war Europe, was portrayed as a national humiliation for Germany, and Adolf Hitler was heralded as the hero destined to restore the nation's honour.

Biology, once a favourite subject of mine, was tainted by discussions of race and eugenics, reinforcing the supposed superiority of Aryans. We were warned of the dangers of racial mixing. Geography lessons focused on *Lebensraum* – living space – teaching us that, as the superior race, it was only natural that we should expand our territory into Eastern Europe.

I knew this obsession with Aryan superiority was simply wrong, but questioning it was not an option. Teachers would not tolerate dissension. Perhaps they feared losing their jobs – or worse – if they allowed students to challenge Nazi ideology. Membership of the National Socialist Teachers' League was mandatory, ensuring that every educator adhered to Party doctrine.

New textbooks reflected this blatant indoctrination, filled with virulent anti-Semitic propaganda. Jews were caricatured as parasites, draining the life out of Germany. Within a year, Jewish children would be banned from German schools altogether.

Physical education, once a source of enjoyment, had become wholly militaristic. Boys spent hours drilling in preparation for future military service, while girls were subjected to rigorous calisthenics to strengthen us for our supposed duty – childbearing. School had become nothing more than an extension of the Hitler Youth.

Religion, meanwhile, was marginalised. Adolf Hitler was elevated to the status of a quasi-religious figure, demanding our absolute loyalty and devotion.

I found myself counting down the days until I could leave. I became more of an observer than a participant, if that makes sense. This detached attitude earned me more than one warning from the school principal.

'Sophie, if you do not demonstrate a more positive attitude towards National Socialism, you risk failing your *Abitur*.'

I simply did not understand what National Socialism had to do with education. The Nazis had damaged learning by banning books written by some of our greatest writers – Thomas Mann, Stefan Zweig, Heinrich Heine, and countless others. Surely, if I completed my assignments and did well in the exams, that should be enough?

Outside school, I sought solace in simple pleasures. At the sight of a meadow bursting with wildflowers, I would run through it like a child. If I came across a clear, running stream, I could never resist the urge to take off my shoes and socks and dip my feet into the cool water. At heart, I was a child of nature. I relished the feel of buttercups brushing against my cheek, the tickle of grass against my skin.

And I had always been fascinated by wildlife. I could sit for hours watching a beetle scramble over my fingers or lie on my back, feeling insects scurry over my bare arms and legs. We are all God's creatures, and I considered it a blessing when these tiny beings chose me as their companion.

My brothers, Hans and Werner, had an older friend named Fritz Hartnagel. I often tagged along when they went hiking or swimming, though Fritz, kind as he was, paid me little attention. To him, I was just Hans's little sister.

Annelies Kammerer's parents owned a gramophone and an impressive collection of modern records – swing, jazz, blues. The kind of music the Nazis despised. That gramophone made Annelies far more popular than she might have been otherwise. One day, in the early autumn of 1937, she invited a group of us to her house for a dance party.

I was enjoying myself, lost in the rhythm, when Annelies leaned in and whispered something in my ear. I didn't catch it over the music.

'What?' I asked.

She cupped a hand to my ear and repeated, louder this time, 'Fritz is watching you.' Then she giggled. Annelies could be very irritating at times.

I instantly became self-conscious and stopped dancing. I had never liked being the centre of attention. Glancing towards Fritz, I caught him looking away just as our eyes met. He blushed.

Until that moment, I had never seen him as anything more than Hans's friend. But now, I noticed his serious expression, the strong line of his dark brows, his neatly parted hair, cut short in military style. He had recently joined the army, and he carried himself with a maturity far beyond the boys in my class at school, who were all either gawkish or spotty.

Before I could talk myself out of it, I crossed the room to him.

'Why have you stopped dancing?' he asked.

'Why were you watching me?' I challenged.

He hesitated, flustered. 'Well, er... because you're a very good dancer.'

Now it was my turn to blush. 'Thank you. Do you want to dance with me?'

'I'd like to,' he admitted, 'but I have to warn you – I'm not very good.'

I liked his honesty. 'I can teach you.' Without thinking, I took his hand and pulled him into the centre of the room, surprised by my own boldness.

He was right – he wasn't a very good dancer. Too stiff, too formal. He struggled to relax into the music. After a few attempts, we gave up, laughing, and went to fetch a couple of beers instead. We sat on a sofa, leaning in close to hear each other over the music. His aftershave lingered in the air – sandalwood with a hint of citrus. I found myself shifting a little closer.

'What made you join the army?' I asked.

'I thought it would be an interesting career,' he said. 'I'm training to be an officer.'

'So what do you think of Hitler?'

His expression hardened. 'My loyalty is to the army. Not to Hitler.' He made the distinction clear. 'And what do you want to do when you leave school?' he asked, changing the subject.

'I plan to go to university.'

'What will you study?'

'Biology and philosophy.'

He raised an eyebrow. 'That's an interesting combination. Why those two?'

'I want to understand how life works,' I explained. 'That's the biology part. And I want to understand how to live a good life. That's the philosophy part.'

He nodded, thoughtful. 'I have no doubt that you will live a very good life, Sophie Scholl.' He held my gaze, and his face broke into a warm smile. My heart did a little somersault.

I wanted to see him again, but he was returning to his regiment in Ulm in a couple of days. Before he left, I promised to write, and he scribbled his address on a scrap of paper for me.

'I shall look forward to your letters,' he said, slipping the paper into my hand.

In the autumn of 1937, Hans completed his six-month stint with the Reich Labour Service, helping to build Hitler's motorways. At first, he had tried to make the best of it. He wrote home, saying he was throwing himself into the work and that it was good for young people to become more independent. That sounded just like Hans. But by the end, he admitted that the work was monotonous. In a letter to Inge, he wrote that in the evenings, they mostly sat around the big table in the barrack room and read. He was relieved when it was over.

Yet, university would have to wait. Now, he had to complete his military service. Hans had always loved horses and riding, so he signed up for the cavalry at Bad Cannstatt, just outside Stuttgart.

His letters from that time suggested life wasn't too bad. He had plenty of time to read, and the army didn't interfere with his choice of books – unlike those fanatics in the Hitler Youth. He also stayed in touch with his friends from the dj.1.11. That should have been harmless, but it would prove disastrous.

The first sign of trouble came with a loud hammering at our apartment door early one November morning. It was still dark outside. I was getting ready for school.

I froze mid-button, listening. Was there a fire? A neighbour in distress? But no one we knew would pound on the door like that. It could only mean one thing.

Father had already left for work. Hans, of course, was in Bad Cannstatt. I joined Inge, Liesl, and Werner in the hallway as Mother went to answer the door.

Two men stood on the landing, their grey, belted raincoats and trilby hats unmistakable. The Gestapo. The secret police.

'We have a warrant to search your apartment,' said the taller one with a moustache.

'On what grounds?' Mother demanded. It was brave of her to question them rather than simply stepping aside.

'We have evidence that your son, Hans Scholl, is involved in an illegal organisation. Now, stand aside, please.'

They pushed past without waiting for permission.

'We will search the house, and then the children will accompany us for questioning.'

'Why the children?' Mother protested.

'We are not obliged to answer your questions.'

I knew it then. They were cracking down on members of the banned dj.1.11. group. They must have known Hans wasn't here, but that didn't matter. Under Nazi logic, if one member of a family was guilty, then everyone was guilty. *Sippenhaft* – clan arrest. A medieval law revived by the Nazis to punish entire families for an individual's so-called crimes. I caught Inge's eye. Perhaps she, too, was thinking of our teacher who had vanished.

Mother remained composed. 'I have to go to the bakery,' she said. 'You may begin your search in the living room.'

'Through here,' Inge said, stepping forward. She had understood Mother's plan better than I had.

As Inge and Liesl led the men into the living room, Mother grabbed a basket from the hallway and hurried into the room Hans shared with Werner. Werner and I followed.

'Quick,' she whispered. 'Find anything suspicious.'

We knew exactly what she meant – Hans's notebooks. Distinctive in their grey and red covers, likely filled with anti-Nazi thoughts. We rifled through drawers and under the bed until we found them. Mother tucked them into her basket and covered them with a clean tea towel. Then she poked her head into the living room, where the officers were rummaging through bookshelves and the writing desk.

'I won't be long,' she said lightly. 'But the baker sells out early.'

They barely acknowledged her as she slipped out, carrying the incriminating evidence in plain sight.

The search continued. When Mother returned, her basket held nothing but a fresh loaf of bread. I wondered what she had done with the notebooks. I later learned she had entrusted them to a neighbour.

Of course, the Gestapo found nothing useful. But they weren't satisfied. They insisted Inge, Werner, and I accompany them for questioning. Only Liesl was spared. At least one of us would stay with Mother, who looked close to tears.

The three of us were bundled into a black car and driven away. A neighbour watched from a window. I held my head high. Being arrested by the Gestapo meant you weren't a supporter of the regime. That was something to be proud of.

They took us to separate rooms. My interrogator barely glanced up from his papers.

'Name!' he barked.

'Scholl.'

'Christian name!'

'Sophie.'

He looked up in surprise. 'What are you doing here?'

'Your colleagues brought me.'

'But you're a girl!' He sounded almost irritated, as if I had tricked him.

'I never said I wasn't.'

'Don't be insolent!'

At the time, I had very short hair and was wearing trousers. Still, it didn't say much for Gestapo powers of observation if they had arrested me thinking I was a boy.

The officer left to consult his superiors. When he returned, he dismissed me. 'You are free to go.'

'What about my brother and sister?' I demanded. 'Are they coming too?'

'No. They are being sent to Stuttgart for further questioning.'

I walked home alone. If Inge and Werner had been with me, we might have laughed about my mistaken identity. But it wasn't funny anymore.

I was furious. What right did these men have to interfere in our lives? If Hans and Werner wanted to go hiking with friends and discuss philosophy, what harm was there in that? And what did it have to do with the rest of us?

Father was right. We were living in a prison. The walls were closing in.

But I would not let it crush me. I straightened my back and walked taller.

That moment, National Socialism died for me.

They held Inge and Werner for a week – the longest week of my life. Mother was beside herself with worry. Liesl and I did what we could to support her. Father was incandescent. He ranted, threatened to break into the prison himself. Mother dissuaded him, knowing it would send him straight to a concentration camp.

Each hour felt like a day, each day like a month.

When Inge and Werner were finally released, we welcomed them with joy in our hearts.

Then the Gestapo arrested Hans.

It was inevitable. His clashes with the Hitler Youth hadn't gone unnoticed. His involvement in dj.1.11. had caught up with him.

He was sent to the remand prison in Stuttgart. They interrogated him for days. Why did he join an illegal organisation? Who else was involved?

Hans could not tell them the truth – that the group had shown him what it meant to truly live. Hiking, reading, debating, music, poetry, philosophy – these things had shaped him. The Hitler Youth had offered only mindless marching and empty rhetoric.

But he couldn't say any of that. He spoke only of camping and literature. His interrogator dismissed it as irrelevant.

'You read banned books!'

'We read books by Germany's greatest writers.'

His captors didn't care.

Father finally secured a visit. When he returned, he told us Hans had apologised for the pain he had caused us.

'I told him we are proud of him,' Father said, all their previous disagreements long forgotten. 'Hans asked for textbooks. He wants to study.'

That was so like him. Even in a prison cell, he refused to be idle.

That evening, we walked along the banks of the Danube with Father. He was in a reflective mood. His visit to Stuttgart had affected him deeply. Suddenly he said, 'If anything happens to any of you, I'll go to Berlin and shoot *that man* myself.'

We loved him for that. He was so strong and steadfast. He was our rock. We felt we were standing on granite.

Christmas was a subdued event that year. Hans was still in prison. We went to church and I prayed fervently for Hans's release. The family wasn't whole without him.

And then, without warning, he was released. The Wehrmacht had intervened. Even with the Gestapo, the military still had influence.

Hans returned to his barracks. But now, he had a Gestapo record. He was a marked man.

Chapter Seven

February 1943

I want to ask Else how she ended up here as a political prisoner, but that conversation will have to wait. The guards return to the cell and take me for another round of questioning with Herr Mohr. I thought he was finished with me for the day, but it seems he is prepared to go on long into the night. As the guards lead me down the corridor, I remember Else's words: *Admit nothing that they can't prove*. I repeat it to myself like a mantra. *Admit nothing that they can't prove*.

I think of Hans and wonder where he is. I pray that he remains strong.

'Sit,' says Mohr, pointing at the chair with his fountain pen. He sits behind his desk, writing something I cannot read upside down, his mouth set in a thin line, his brow furrowed in concentration.

It's dark outside now. I wonder what our friends are doing at this moment. Has anyone managed to get word to our parents in Ulm about our arrest? I sense it's going to be a long night. I take my seat, back straight, hands folded in my lap, and wait for the interrogation to begin.

Mohr lights a cigarette but, this time, doesn't offer me one. Is it my imagination, or does he seem grimmer than before? Has he uncovered new evidence?

He exhales a long plume of smoke. 'My men have been to 23 Franz-Joseph Strasse 13.'

My stomach clenches. He means the apartment Hans and I share – the one we rent from Frau Schmidt, who is currently away in the countryside, avoiding the British bombs. Our home in Munich. Was it really only this morning that we left for the university, expecting to return by lunchtime? It feels like another lifetime. I left the breakfast dishes in the sink, water still in the samovar. Did I leave my room tidy? The thought of Gestapo agents rifling through my drawers, fingering my books, scrutinising my records makes me feel sick. *Schubert's Trout Quintet* is still on the phonograph. What right do they have to invade my space? I feel violated.

At least we were careful. The typewriter and mimeograph machine are not in the apartment. We keep them in Manfred Eickemeyer's studio. I wait to see what Mohr will say next.

'My men conducted a thorough search,' Mohr continues, 'and we found a large batch of eight-pfennig stamps.'

I swallow hard. The stamps. They were in my desk drawer. I had bought them in small batches from different locations, careful not to attract attention. We needed them to post our leaflets across Munich and beyond.

Mohr leans forward. 'Why do you need so many stamps?'

'I write a lot of letters to my friends and family.' It's true. I've always been a devoted letter-writer – letters to my parents, to my siblings, and especially to Fritz Hartnagel, though I haven't heard from him in some time. The last I knew, he was in Russia, suffering from frostbite. I miss him desperately.

Mohr doesn't look convinced. Then he pushes a piece of paper across the desk. It is the letter Hans tried to destroy in Dr Wüst's office. The Gestapo has pieced it back together like a jigsaw. The ink is smudged, but the words are still legible.

'This,' Mohr says, tapping the paper, 'reads just like the other leaflets we have collected. Six different leaflets in total. Well?'

'I don't recognise the handwriting.'

'Don't lie to me!' His voice is sharp. 'We found another letter in your brother's room – from someone called Christoph Probst.'

My stomach lurches.

'We compared the handwriting to this.' He gestures to the reconstructed letter. 'It matches exactly. Do you know what that means?'

I do. Christoph Probst. My heart twists at the thought of him. He warned Hans not to take leaflets to the university – not in writing, of course, but face to face. He is in Innsbruck with the Luftwaffe, his wife gravely ill after childbirth. He has no idea what has happened to us. No way of knowing that he, too, is in danger. Our friends in Munich – Alex, Willi, Traute, Professor Huber – they will understand immediately and take precautions. But Christoph...

Mohr, triumphant, takes another paper from his folder. 'I have here a confession from your brother, Hans. Let me read it to you.'

Is he bluffing? My pulse pounds as I wait for him to speak.

Mohr adjusts his reading glasses and begins. '"After I realised that it was impossible for us to win the war, I knew that the only option was to shorten it. I hated the way we treated the people in the lands we occupied."'

'That is just a political opinion,' I say. 'It has nothing to do with the leaflets.'

Mohr ignores me. 'We are talking about troop demoralisation and high treason!'

'I don't believe Hans said those things.'

Mohr's face darkens. 'You dare to accuse me of lying?'

I am exhausted. It is getting harder to think straight.

Then, his voice sharp: 'Eickemeyer's studio!'

My breath catches. They have found it. But how? Some clue left in the apartment? A careless mistake?

'What about it?' I ask, keeping my tone neutral.

'You have a key.'

'Herr Eickemeyer is working as an architect in Kraków,' I say. 'He gave us a key so we could keep an eye on the place and show his pictures to our friends.'

Mohr's gaze is fixed on me. 'There is a copying machine in the studio. Your brother's fingerprints are all over it.'

The silence stretches. The stenographer's fingers hover over her machine, waiting.

I force myself to stay calm. 'Hans must have touched the copying machine while we were there.'

Mohr studies me, almost pitying. 'Your brother has confessed to everything.'

The ground seems to drop beneath me.

'Hans claims he wrote, copied, and distributed all six leaflets. Thousands of copies. Alone. I have his signed confession.' He slides a typed page towards me. Hans's signature is at the bottom.

Oh, Hans. What have they forced you to do? But I see his strategy – he is trying to protect us. To take all the blame himself. Except, Mohr doesn't believe him.

'You live with your brother. Do you really expect us to believe you know nothing?' He leans forward. 'You were with him at the university this morning. Did you really think those leaflets were harmless? Admit it! You and your brother did this together!'

Hans cannot take all the blame. I will not let him. We are in this together, and I am proud of that.

'Yes,' I say, meeting Mohr's gaze. 'My brother and I did this together. No one else was involved.'

Mohr's expression remains doubtful. I know he doesn't believe me.

Chapter Eight

1938

It was January, and the air outside was bitterly cold. The schoolyard lay beneath a thick layer of snow, but inside the classroom, I sat bored, my thoughts far from the lesson. Instead, I was thinking of Fritz Hartnagel, still stationed in Augsburg. When the teacher wasn't looking, I slipped a piece of writing paper into the back of my exercise book and began composing a letter to him. I had been writing to him since the previous autumn, and, to my delight, he always responded, seeming to enjoy even the most trivial things I told him.

I wrote about Annelies Kammerer, who had suffered a concussion after falling and hitting her head, and now, in her usual clumsy way, had broken her fibula. There was another dance party coming up in a few weeks, and I hoped he would be able to attend. And if he could get leave, he might even accompany me to the Red Cross Ball in Stuttgart the following week. I worried that he might be lonely in Augsburg and joked that when Annelies recovered, we would hike there to visit him – though only when the weather was warmer.

Imagine my joy when I received his reply, thanking me for the invitation and promising to join me if he could get leave.

Two weeks later, in another dull lesson, I wrote to him again. His twenty-first birthday was approaching on the fourth of February, and I wanted to wish him a happy birthday. He was four years older than me, but I teased that in four years, I would catch up. I told him how much I was looking forward to seeing him in Ulm soon.

That year, I was more excited than ever for the annual *Fasching* Carnival parade before Lent. Fritz was due back in town, and I imagined us enjoying the festivities together. The *Münsterplatz* was crowded with families and children, drawn to the spectacle of fools and jesters in their vibrant costumes, the witches with their straw wigs and grotesque masks, the devils with horns and dark fur, their fearsome wooden faces leering at the crowd.

I scanned the sea of people, searching for Fritz.

'Sophie!'

I turned at the sound of his voice – and found him standing with a woman clinging to his arm. My stomach dropped. In that moment, I wished I were wearing a mask to hide my shock and disappointment. I reminded myself that I had no claim on Fritz. We were just friends, nothing more. I forced a smile, though it felt strained.

'How are you enjoying the parade?' he asked.

'Great,' I lied.

His companion smiled at me. I recognised her immediately – she worked at the bookshop where I had once bought a novel. There was an awkward silence. She must have wondered why Fritz was speaking to a teenage girl. The crowd jostled around us, making the moment even more unbearable. Fritz and I exchanged pleasantries about our families, but before I could find a graceful way to leave, his companion spotted someone she knew and dragged him away. It was all terribly awkward. I left the parade soon afterward and tried to read a book at home, but I couldn't focus on the words.

In my next letter to Fritz, I told him about a dream I'd had. In it, I was camping by a lake when a woman took me out in a boat under the moonlight. The moon was an enormous pale disc, illuminating the water's surface. Far in the distance, a small red dot shone through the clouds. The woman explained that it was the sun – that we were in the only place in the world where the sun and moon could be seen together.

'I like to dream,' I wrote. 'I live in a strange world where I'm never really happy.' Then, worried he might think me sentimental, I quickly added, 'But I'm actually very materialistic. For example, the woman you were with at *Fasching* sold me a book for less than it was worth.'

I wished I could visit him in Augsburg and lamented how far away it seemed. Eighty-five kilometres – yet it might as well have been eight hundred.

What drivel I wrote. And yet, he never complained.

> *I'm in a bad temper. I pinched some of Liesl's writing paper. I bit through Inge's necklace!*
>
> *I'm in a foul mood today! It's so cold I can't go out! Don't you dare laugh at me!*
>
> *Are you ever irritated by the tripe I write? Anger makes people old and ugly.*

As soon as the weather improved, I convinced my friend Lisa Remppis to take a trip with me to Augsburg to visit Fritz. We took the train and, once we arrived, found a payphone to call his barracks. A pompous-sounding man answered.

I couldn't speak for laughing, and Lisa grabbed the handset from me.

'Hello,' Lisa said. 'Could I speak to Lieutenant Har—' She broke off, dissolving into giggles so that *Hartnagel* came out as *Ha-Ha-Ha*.

'Lieutenant Who?' the voice demanded.

I took the phone from her, elbowing her ribs. 'Lieutenant Hartnagel,' I managed between giggles. She poked me back.

'One moment, please,' said the voice at the other end.

We held our breath, fearing they would hang up on us. But then–

'Hello?'

My heart leapt at the sound of Fritz's voice. 'Hello! It's me, Sophie. I'm in Augsburg with Lisa.'

'What are you doing here?' He sounded surprised but not displeased.

'I told you I would visit! Didn't you believe me?'

'Well, no – I mean, yes.'

'Can we see you?'

'Of course. Where are you now?'

'At the train station.'

'Give me twenty minutes.'

We waited, stamping our feet against the cold. Finally, Fritz arrived in an army vehicle.

'Get in,' he said, opening the door. 'You know this is completely against the rules, don't you?'

'We won't be any trouble,' I promised, grinning.

Fritz smuggled us into his room and, to our delight, brought food from the kitchen. I was so happy that he hadn't turned us away. We talked and laughed late into the night. When it was time to sleep, he let Lisa and me share his bed while he took the armchair.

The next morning, he sneaked us out again, and we caught the train back to Ulm.

It had been completely reckless – and completely wonderful.

On the first of April 1938, Hitler visited Stuttgart. Hans's regiment was assigned to mount a guard of honour, welcoming the Führer to the city. Swastika banners hung from lampposts, and throngs of enthusiastic supporters lined the streets, leaning out of upstairs windows to give the Nazi salute and cheer as Hitler's open-top Mercedes crawled past. Standing upright in the car, he returned their salutes with his usual theatrical precision. It was yet another spectacle of Nazi self-glorification.

Hitler had recently returned from Austria, basking in the success of the annexation, and the jubilation of the crowd reflected what they saw as a great triumph for Germany.

The Austrian Chancellor, Kurt Schuschnigg, had intended to hold a referendum on whether Austria should remain independent or become part of the German Reich. But the day before the vote was scheduled, German troops marched across the border. Schuschnigg was forced to resign, and the Austrian government collapsed. In Vienna, Hitler was greeted by throngs of ecstatic supporters, the streets flooded with swastika flags and chants of *Heil Hitler!* The newspapers called it a homecoming. Father called it an invasion.

Hans's regiment had not been part of the military operation in Austria. Like the rest of us, he listened to the frenzied celebrations on the radio. In a letter home, he expressed his unease, wondering where it would all end. He admitted that he no longer understood people – their blind enthusiasm, their overwhelming joy at what had happened. The crowds, the hysteria, the flags and salutes – it all left him bewildered. It made him want to escape, to walk alone in a vast, open plain where he could be free from it all.

I knew exactly how he felt. We were alike in so many ways.

I was overjoyed when Fritz remembered my birthday in May. It fell on a Monday that year, and I had turned seventeen. But in my letter to him the following day, I couldn't resist teasing him just a little. I told him how I had waited for him to arrive on Saturday, and when he hadn't come, I had gone to the May Dance with a boy from school – Oskar Stammler. I didn't particularly care for Oskar, but he was available, and Fritz wasn't, and I had wanted to dance.

Was I trying to make Fritz a little jealous, just as I had been when I saw him at *Fasching* with that other woman? I wasn't proud of such sentiments, but I wanted him to notice me.

My letter must have had an effect because he soon wrote back, saying he would be in Ulm on the weekend of the twenty-first and twenty-second and hoped I would be free to see him. Of course, I told him I would be delighted. As the weekend approached, I anticipated his arrival with the excitement of a small child awaiting Christmas.

When the long-awaited Saturday arrived, I was up early, too restless to sleep. The sun was shining, mirroring my mood. Fritz was coming to Ulm, and he wanted to see me. We met in the centre of town, by the leaning Metzger Tower, and at first, we were almost shy with each other. As we strolled along the river, he asked after my family, and I asked about life in Augsburg. It was strange – I had poured out my thoughts and feelings to him in letter after letter, but now that he was here beside me, I found myself tongue-tied.

Summoning my courage, I enquired as casually as I could whether he planned to see the woman from the bookshop while he was in town. My heart pounded as I waited for his response.

'I came to see you, Sophie,' he said, his hand brushing against mine. A tingling sensation ran up my arm and down my spine. 'I've been thinking about you a lot.'

'And I've been thinking about you,' I admitted.

Our fingers entwined as we walked, and a wave of happiness rushed over me. Finding a quiet spot on the riverbank, we sat down together. Then he kissed me, and I kissed him back. I laughed out of sheer joy, and then we were in each other's arms, exploring each other's mouths with our tongues. The sensation of his strong arms around me, pulling me close, was intoxicating. I had never felt anything so glorious. Time seemed to stop – we forgot the hour, forgot everything but each other.

When hunger finally reminded us of reality, we realised we had missed dinner. We went to a cosy inn and ordered steaming bowls of potato soup with smoked sausage. Even then, neither of us wanted the night to end. We stayed out late, walking, talking – and kissing. The day melted into night, and I barely noticed.

By the time I returned home, it was the early hours of the morning. I crept into bed as quietly as I could, trying not to wake anyone.

Fritz had to leave for Augsburg on Sunday, but we promised to write.

The next morning, I was still lost in dreams when Liesl shook me awake. 'Sophie, it's time to get up!'

In my confusion, I thought she was just getting into bed herself. But then I saw the daylight streaming through the curtains. I had slept half the morning, and Mother was worried about me. Pulling the covers up to my chin, I closed my eyes again, determined to savour the memory of the previous day just a little longer.

May marked the beginning of the most perfect summer. Nearly every day, I swam in the Iller with Werner and a group of friends. Water has always felt like my natural element – I loved the sensation of gliding through it, the rush of exhilaration as I pushed myself to swim faster. I felt alive, free. Afterwards, we would stretch out on the riverbank, drying ourselves in the sun. Whenever Fritz had leave, he joined us, and then we would slip away to spend precious moments alone.

Our relationship was constrained by the demands of his military career. He was always sweet and patient with me, but at times, I sensed that he wanted more than I was prepared to give. He was four years older, after all. I cared for him deeply, but I wasn't ready to cross that threshold. I didn't want to disappoint him, yet I also knew I had to stay true to myself.

That summer, Inge was working as a governess for a family in Lesum, just outside Bremen. She wrote to say that her employers had extended an open invitation to any friends or family of hers who wished to visit. Werner and I were immediately interested, and I also invited Lisa Remppis and Annelies Kammerer. Herr Kammerer kindly offered to drive us, and we gratefully accepted. We arranged to go in July. Unfortunately, Hans couldn't join us – he was still stationed in Bad Cannstatt with his cavalry regiment. But love must have been in the air that summer, because not only was I dating Fritz, but Hans had started visiting Lisa in Leonberg on weekends, and the two of them were now going out together.

Fritz, however, couldn't join us in Bremen. He was set to be transferred to Vienna in August, and I hated the thought of him leaving.

We spent a few days in Bremen with Inge's employers, the Eggers family, who had two daughters, Susi and Annelieschen, eighteen and sixteen. Then we all set off for the North Sea.

I fell in love with the North Sea instantly. After the mountains and valleys of the south, the landscape was so open, so vast – you could see for miles in every direction. And the sea! I had never known such exhilaration as when I swam in its wild, crashing waves.

One morning, we set out on a fishing trip. Lisa and I boarded one trawler, while Inge, Annelies, and Werner took another. At the last minute, four Hitler Youth leaders and a married couple joined our boat because their fisherman had fallen ill. I wasn't pleased – they were intruders in our little adventure – but there was no arguing with circumstances.

The sky was ink-black when we set off, not a single star visible. But as we sailed beyond the East Frisian Islands, the first light of dawn broke over the horizon. It was glorious, though the wind bit into our skin. The wife of the married couple was dreadfully seasick, and I'm ashamed to say we weren't very sympathetic. We hadn't wanted them on our boat in the first place.

The Hitler Youth boys, however, turned out to be all right once we got talking. They were eager to flirt with us, and we didn't exactly discourage them.

When the fishermen hauled in the nets, I was mesmerised by the wriggling fish, the scuttling crabs, the starfish clinging stubbornly to the netting. The fishermen wasted no time boiling the large crabs, and the stench was awful. We sang sea shanties until, to my mortification, I ended up seasick over the side of the boat. It served me right for laughing at the poor woman earlier.

After that, I curled up on the deck and let the gentle rocking of the boat lull me to sleep. It was blissful.

The summer seemed to fly by, and before I knew it, August was drawing to a close. I refused to let go of those final golden days, savouring every moment. On the last morning of the school holidays, I lay in bed until nearly midday, writing a long letter to Fritz.

Looking back now on the summer of '38, I ask myself – did I have any sense that what we were enjoying couldn't last? I honestly don't know. I was young, in love, and happy to be alive.

But storm clouds were gathering on the horizon.

Father kept himself well-informed about events in Germany and abroad. Despite the Nazis' ban on foreign radio stations, he frequently tuned in to the BBC, making his usual wry remark after dinner: 'Now, if you'll excuse me, I'll go and earn myself a prison sentence.'

It was his little joke.

But really, it was no laughing matter.

Joseph Goebbels, Hitler's Reich Minister of Propaganda, controlled all approved radio broadcasts. Father had long since lost any trust in a government that interfered with personal freedoms. He relied on the BBC for an unbiased perspective on world affairs.

In September, the big news was the meeting in Munich. The participants: Adolf Hitler, British Prime Minister Neville Chamberlain, French Premier Édouard Daladier, and, as Father put it, 'that trumped-up fool of an Italian,' Benito Mussolini. The topic? Hitler's plan to annex the German-speaking Sudetenland from Czechoslovakia – just as he had annexed Austria earlier in the year. Strangely, no one thought to invite the Czechoslovaks to the meeting that would decide their fate.

Hitler assured the world that once he had the Sudetenland, his territorial ambitions would be satisfied. Eager to avoid another war, the other leaders agreed. Czechoslovakia was given no say in the matter. Chamberlain returned to Britain to rapturous applause, famously proclaiming as he stepped off the plane that the agreement was 'a prelude to peace in Europe.'

Father was livid. 'Hitler promised not to make any further territorial claims,' he scoffed, 'and Chamberlain believed him!'

The next day, German troops marched into the Sudetenland. No one in our family was surprised when, a few months later, they occupied the rest of Czechoslovakia as well.

And then came one of the most shocking nights of my life. Even now, the memory churns my stomach.

It was a Wednesday in November, bitterly cold and dark. Inside, we were sheltered from the chill, warmed by the soft glow of the lamps. I spent the evening reading while Liesl played the piano. Hans had completed his basic military service and was now in Tübingen, serving a six-month stint as a medic in an army hospital – a prerequisite for studying medicine at university. Inge was still working for the family in Bremen. As always, Father was in his study, listening to foreign radio stations, defying the government's ban.

When my eyes grew too tired to focus on the words of my book, I closed it and climbed into bed. Sleep came quickly.

I awoke with a start.

Outside, voices shouted in anger, surging through the darkness. I sat up, heart pounding, and went to the window.

Münsterplatz was swarming with Storm Troopers, the so-called Brownshirts, alongside teenage boys from the Hitler Youth. They marched with torches, their faces lit by flickering flames. Their chanting rose in a frenzied roar. They were calling for the Jews. Some wielded hammers and iron bars.

A sick feeling lodged in my chest. This wasn't a rally. This was a mob.

Moments later, the sky glowed with eerie orange light. Flames leapt from the direction of Weinhof – the location of the Jewish synagogue. Then came the unmistakable sound of shattering glass.

The bedroom door creaked open. Father stood in his dressing gown, his expression grave, his shoulders weighed with an invisible burden.

'Come away from the window, Sophie. It's not safe.'

I obeyed. But sleep never returned.

The next morning, we learned that the violence had not been confined to Ulm. Across Germany, from Berlin to Munich, synagogues had burned. Jewish-owned shops and businesses were looted and destroyed. Thousands of Jewish men had been arrested and sent to Dachau.

Kristallnacht.

The Night of Broken Glass.

It was nothing short of government-sanctioned terror.

The attack had been orchestrated. A month earlier, 17,000 Polish Jews had been forcibly deported from Germany, only to be stranded at the Polish border. Poland refused to take them. Among the deportees was the family of a young man living in Paris. Enraged by his father's treatment, the seventeen-year-old sought revenge. He entered the German Embassy in Paris, intending to assassinate the German Ambassador to France. But the ambassador was unavailable. Instead, he shot a low-ranking diplomat, Ernst vom Rath.

Joseph Goebbels seized the opportunity. The Nazi propaganda machine claimed that International Jewry was conspiring against Germany. The call went out for retribution.

And so the Reich avenged itself on its own defenceless citizens.

The next day, an article in the *Ulm Daily* described the violence as 'the justified anger of the populace.' The report concluded with chilling finality: 'Although the removal of Jews from Ulm has made great progress since the takeover of power, we intend that through our discipline, the rest of the Jewish rabble will leave our town even more quickly.'

The synagogue had been destroyed.

Even now, it is difficult to articulate the emotions that consumed me then – rage at the brutality, shame at my own helplessness. The fear I felt for my Jewish friends. Luise Nathan's father was arrested and sent to Dachau. He was later released, but the message was clear: leave, or risk something far worse.

Within months, the Nathans fled to England.

Father had been right all along. Hitler was waging war against his own people. The dream of the Fatherland was dead.

Chapter Nine

February 1943

M ohr dismisses me, and the guards escort me back to the cell I share with Else. They bring us a meagre meal of bread and soup. It's late, and I'm starving, so I tuck in without hesitation. It has been a long, gruelling day. But despite my exhaustion, sleep is out of the question. My mind is too wired, my nerves too taut.

I turn to Else. 'Tell me about yourself.'

She puts down her spoon and studies me for a moment, as if weighing how much to reveal. Then she speaks. 'I was born in Augsburg, in Bavaria. Do you know it?'

'Kind of.'

I don't tell her that I went there once to post leaflets – no time to admire the cathedral, the town hall, or the medieval houses. I had been too busy skulking through the dark streets, heart hammering, stuffing leaflets into letterboxes and hoping to avoid the Gestapo. My task had been clear: distribute as many as possible, then board the next train back to Munich without drawing attention to myself. I had succeeded. But there had been no sightseeing.

'Do you have brothers or sisters?' I ask.

'Two brothers, Willy and Arno,' she says, and a flicker of warmth enters her voice. 'But no sisters. I shared an apartment with Willy.'

'Like me and Hans.'

A sharp pang of longing strikes me. I wish the Gestapo would let me see Hans. I wonder what they are doing to him, whether he is safe, whether he is holding firm. My heart aches at the thought of my family. They must know about the arrests by now. Someone will have told them.

'And your parents?' I ask.

She sighs. 'Mother died when I was twenty. It was hard for us.'

'I'm sorry.'

My own mother suffers from heart problems, and I dread to think how she will bear the news of our arrest. I push the thought aside. I can't afford to dwell on it now.

Else lowers her voice. 'My brothers and I were vehemently opposed to the Nazis.'

I nod. It is good to hear it spoken aloud, to know I am not alone. There are others who see the truth.

'I worked as a secretary for the Jewish owner of a department store in Munich,' she continues. 'Until *Kristallnacht*.'

She pauses, lost in memory. I too remember that horrific night in November 1938. The images of broken glass and burning buildings are seared into my mind.

'They destroyed the shop,' Else says at last. 'Looted everything, then set it on fire.'

'What happened to the owner?'

'The whole family was taken to Dachau.'

Dachau. The very name is enough to send ice through my veins. The same camp where the teacher from Ulm disappeared. The same place where countless others have vanished. The truth of what happens behind the barbed wire remains a mystery, but the fear of it looms over us all.

'So what did you do?' I ask. 'After Kristallnacht?'

She straightens her back, steel entering her gaze. 'My brothers and I joined a communist resistance group. We thought it was the best way to fight Nazism.'

I wish I had known her before. She would have fitted in with the White Rose. Her quiet resolve, her ordinariness hiding a core of strength, would have made her one of us.

'How did you end up here?' I ask.

Else shakes her head. 'Who knows? Maybe someone betrayed us. Or maybe the Gestapo infiltrated the group. They have eyes and ears everywhere.'

A heavy silence settles between us. Then, from the corridor outside, the rhythmic stomp of boots. The sound echoes through the prison like an omen.

Chapter Ten

1939

As 1938 drew to a close, I found myself grappling with self-doubt about my relationship with Fritz. Looking back, I realise this uncertainty stemmed more from my own shifting emotions than from anything he had done. Fritz remained steadfast, patient, and kind. But I am not good with winter. The long, dark months, confined indoors, leave me restless and irritable. I crave fresh air and movement, and without them, I feel trapped.

Maintaining a relationship with someone you rarely see is not easy. Letters can never replace real conversation. There is no spontaneous exchange, no interruptions, no teasing or playful arguments. No immediate reaction to what you say. And then there are the delays. If Fritz didn't reply to one of my letters straight away, I was gripped with anxiety. Had my letter gone astray? Had I said something to upset him? Was he losing interest in me?

I longed for clarity. What did we really mean to each other? Did we have a future together? Perhaps other girls my age – after all, I was still only seventeen – took a more relaxed approach to love. They lived in the moment, enjoying their time with a boyfriend without questioning what it all meant. But I was not like that. I sought meaning in everything. And yet, while I yearned for certainty, I also feared commitment. I needed Fritz, but I didn't want to feel tied down.

It didn't help that I was growing increasingly frustrated with school. National Socialist doctrine had infiltrated every lesson, distorting subjects I had once loved. Some days, I fantasised about abandoning it all to become a painter. When I had visited Inge the previous summer, we had spent time at the artists' colony in Worpswede. Their way of life had captivated me – living close to nature, painting, writing, and surrounding yourself with people who shared your passions. It seemed a world away from the oppressive, stifling reality of Nazi Germany.

Fritz, ever patient, never pressured me. He reassured me that he expected nothing I was unwilling to give. The trouble was, I didn't know what I wanted.

We spent time together over New Year, and being with him settled my restless mind. He had an ease about him, a straightforwardness that anchored me. When we were together, my emotional turmoil faded. But our moments together were fleeting. Duty always called him back to his regiment.

In March, Liesl graduated from the Fröbel Seminar, where she had trained as a kindergarten teacher. As a reward for her hard work, our parents gifted her 50 Reichsmarks. To celebrate, she invited me to join her on a skiing trip in Schindelberg in early April. We set off in high spirits, excited for our holiday. But soon after we checked into our hotel, the money vanished. Stolen. We couldn't prove anything, but the result was the same – we were stranded with no means to pay our way.

I wrote to Fritz, asking if he could lend us some money to tide us over. Instead of replying, he arrived the next day and insisted on covering all our expenses.

'We can't let him pay for everything,' Liesl whispered to me that evening. 'It doesn't feel right.'

I agreed, but there was no arguing with Fritz.

'Just tell him you'll pay him back once you start working,' I said.

The skiing did me good. The crisp mountain air and the exhilaration of speeding down the slopes shook off the last of my winter melancholy. I reminded myself that I needed to get outside more. Now that spring was approaching, I had no excuse not to.

Fritz had been transferred to Munich, which meant he would be closer. We would see more of each other. As the days grew longer and the air warmer, my spirits lifted. I stepped into spring with a renewed sense of optimism.

'Have you remembered to pack enough underwear and socks?' Mother asked, carrying a neatly folded pile of freshly laundered shirts into Hans's bedroom.

Hans barely looked up, wrestling with an overflowing suitcase. 'I'll manage,' he muttered, shoving books into every available space before sighing in frustration. 'This is impossible. Nothing fits.'

I leaned against the doorframe, arms crossed, watching his struggle with amusement. 'Maybe you don't need to take the entire contents of your bookshelf with you?'

Hans shot me a glare. 'I like my own books.'

'Don't they have libraries in Munich?' Werner chimed in, sprawled on his bed, flipping through a magazine.

Hans ignored him and tried a different approach, stacking the books in a tighter formation.

I smirked. 'How will you find time to read all those? Won't you be going to lectures all day and drinking beer with friends all night?'

Mother shot me a warning look, but Hans only grinned. 'I'll make time.'

It was April 1939, and at last, Hans was leaving for university, now aged twenty. He had served in the Reich Labour Service, then completed his military training. But now, he was finally heading to the Ludwig Maximilian University in Munich to study medicine – a path he had chosen for himself, rather than one dictated by the state. I planned to follow him as soon as I could.

The previous summer, he had been stationed with his regiment in Stetten on the Bodensee. His letters home spoke of an almost dreamlike existence, untouched by politics. He spent his free time riding through the rolling countryside, avoiding newspapers and the mindless chatter of his comrades, who spoke of war as though it were inevitable. Then, in order to qualify for medical school, he had to attend an army medical corps course in Tübingen. His letters from there had been more animated – he wrote about attending his first autopsy and watching surgeries without fainting, which he considered an accomplishment. Despite missing Christmas in Ulm for the second year in a row, he hadn't minded. He was doing something meaningful, caring for the sick, and that, he wrote, made it all worthwhile.

And now, he was leaving again. I would miss him.

'You have to promise to write,' I told him as he wrestled with his suitcase one last time. 'I want to hear all about your life in Munich.'

Hans grinned at me. 'I promise. But first, you have to help me pack. I can't do this alone.'

He left on the morning train, and the house felt strangely empty without him.

But before the end of the first week, a letter arrived, addressed to Mother and Father.

'Can I read it, please?' I asked eagerly.

Father handed it to me over the breakfast table. I tore it open and scanned the lines as I sipped my coffee.

Dear Parents,

I'm so happy here. I'm coming to life again. So far the best lecture was one on botany. But I'm also enjoying zoology. I've put my name down for so many classes, people will think I'm crazy. I'm also loving Greek and philosophy. Could you find a second-hand edition of Nietzsche for me please? And I should also get a copy of Plato.

Your Loving Son,

Hans.

I stared at the page. 'I thought he was going there to study medicine.'

Father chuckled. 'At this rate, he'll be the best-read doctor in Germany.'

'As long as he still remembers how to cure people.'

Mother tapped my arm. 'Shouldn't you be getting ready for school?'

I sighed and pushed my chair back. 'All right, all right, I'm going.'

But as I gathered my things, I couldn't help thinking of Hans, free to explore whatever ideas fascinated him, while I remained stuck in school. I envied him. I envied his independence, his intellectual freedom.

And I couldn't wait to join him.

I spent my eighteenth birthday in bed with a sore throat. Fritz was away on reconnaissance exercises in the Ziller Valley in Austria, but he still found time to write me a few lines the day before, ensuring his letter arrived on the morning of my birthday.

> *I've just returned from scouting tomorrow's route, and it's already past eleven. But since tomorrow is your birthday, you should know that you will be in my thoughts all day. From the moment I wake to the moment I sleep, whenever I experience something beautiful or joyful, I will imagine telling you about it – that will make it twice as lovely. And if anything troubles me, I will picture you here beside me, and the burden will seem lighter.*
> *Dear Sophie, you have saved me from so much. For that, I would like to thank you.*
> *I only wish I could send you more than this note of gratitude.*

A small wooden crate arrived later that day, packed with wood shavings and crumpled newspaper. Inside was a perfectly carved wooden dolphin. There was no note, but I knew it was from Fritz. He knew exactly what I would like. I ran my fingers over its smooth curves, remembering summer days swimming in the river, feeling as free as the creatures of the water.

The next day, still feeling wretched, I wrote back to him. My illness made me self-pitying and sentimental.

> *Thank you so much for your dear letter. If only I could find the words to tell you everything that I feel. I am forever grateful to you. I sometimes think I take too much from you, always so gladly and so selfishly.*
> *I hope you don't expect too much from me. I would hate to disappoint you.*

A few weeks later, as rain pounded against my bedroom window, another letter from Fritz arrived. He was in Munich, making careful plans for his summer leave. He had long dreamed of travelling to Yugoslavia – to see the Dalmatian Coast, then on to Lake Ohrid via Albania – but he worried that he might have to go alone.

I knew then and there that I wanted to go with him. He hadn't asked, assuming my parents would disapprove of us travelling together. But I was now eighteen. While I wanted my parents' blessing, there was little they could do to stop me.

At the end of June, Fritz sent me a detailed itinerary titled 'First Trip to the Heart of the Balkans.'

We were to leave on the twenty-second of July, travelling from Munich to Salzburg. The next day, we'd reach Trieste and take a bus to Fiume before sailing through the island-studded Adriatic to Dubrovnik. After exploring the old city, we would drive inland, passing through towns and villages, heading south to Lake Ohrid before circling back to the coast. From there, we'd visit Venice and Verona before returning to Munich via the Brenner Pass.

It was an ambitious itinerary, nineteen days of adventure and discovery. Nineteen days in which we would truly get to know each other, instead of piecing together moments stolen between military duty and family obligations. I was excited—*and* a little apprehensive.

Then disaster struck.

The Nazis imposed a foreign exchange embargo and banned young people from travelling abroad. Every hour Fritz had spent carefully mapping our journey had been in vain.

With hindsight, it is easy to see what should have been obvious – Germany was preparing for war. But at eighteen, your world is still small, and my first reaction was selfish frustration. My dreams of wandering through sun-drenched landscapes with Fritz were shattered by bureaucratic decree.

Determined not to let the summer slip away in disappointment, I proposed an alternative – *if we could not travel south, then we would travel north.* Perhaps, subconsciously, I was trying to recreate the magic of the previous summer.

We set off for Heiligenhafen on the Baltic coast, then moved on to the North Sea. Each day was spent in the water, tumbling through the waves. I loved the exhilaration of it, the salty air, the pull of the tides. Later, we visited the artists' colony at Worpswede, near Bremen. I fell in love with the paintings of Paula Modersohn-Becker – her art was raw, honest, full of intensity. I wrote to Inge in a fit of enthusiasm, marvelling at the way Modersohn-Becker portrayed women with such depth and truth. Of course, the Nazis had labelled her work 'degenerate,' but then, the Nazis had no taste.

That summer was a precious time for Fritz and me. We spent our days swimming, walking, or exploring exhibitions. In the evening, we lay in each other's arms, talking about the future. We spoke of marriage once I had finished my studies. We were happy. We were in love.

But summer never lasts.

Fritz was recalled to his regiment. I returned home to Ulm. And the world around us was changing.

Hitler still called himself a *man of peace,* but you only had to look around to see war looming on the horizon. In August, rationing began. Food, shoes, clothes, even soap and coal – all required coupons. Petrol was scarce. We were ordered to keep our curtains drawn at night in preparation for air raids.

Then came the greatest shock of all.

Germany – so long a sworn enemy of the Soviet Union – signed a non-aggression pact with the Bolsheviks. Ribbentrop and Molotov shook hands over a treaty that stunned the world. Stalin, it seemed, was as much a fool as Neville Chamberlain.

Everything felt different now.

War was about to intervene in our lives and turn everything upside down.

Hans had planned to spend the summer in Ulm, but the state had other ideas. Like all students, he was required to work for the Reich in order to continue his studies. That summer, the government ordered students to assist in bringing in the harvest, so Hans was sent to Masuria in East Prussia to work on a 200-acre farm.

His letters home described the relentless labour – long days in the fields, the heat of the sun on his back, the strain in his muscles – but he made the best of it. The beauty of the Masurian countryside, with its vast fields, deep forests, and shimmering lakes, was a welcome escape from the city. And there were compensations. The farmer owned several horses, and Hans was allowed to ride them whenever he liked, which delighted him.

Still, he had his complaints. 'The work is hard, but the worst thing is the stench!' he wrote. 'I can't get close to any of the local girls because they never bathe! I keep myself clean by swimming in the lake, but they don't seem to have discovered the benefits of water yet.'

Evenings were spent around the long wooden table in the farmhouse kitchen, the air thick with the scent of pipe smoke and spirits. Over shots of schnapps, the East Prussians talked freely about their anxieties. For centuries, they had lived with the constant fear of invasion from the east, the memory of Cossack raids never far from their minds. They were fiercely loyal to Germany but felt vulnerable, stranded beyond the Danzig Corridor – the strip of land that gave Poland access to the Baltic, severing East Prussia from the rest of the Reich. Hans wrote that nearly everyone he met in Masuria agreed on one thing: *Hitler had to do something about it.*

And then he did.

On Friday, 1 September 1939, German troops crossed the Polish border. I was at school in Ulm when we heard the news. Hans was still in Masuria.

The next day, Liesl and I walked along the Danube, the water reflecting the grey sky above. She sighed, kicking at a stone with the toe of her shoe. 'I hope there won't be a war,' she said.

I shook my head. 'I hope there will be a war,' I replied, the words coming out more forcefully than I had intended. 'Someone has to stand up to Hitler.'

The very next day, on the third of September, Britain and France declared war on Germany.

The world we knew changed forever.

Mother and Father were frantic with worry about Hans, trapped in East Prussia. War had broken out, and he was in the most exposed corner of the Reich. But Hans has always had the luck of the devil. He managed to catch the very last ship across the Baltic, making it home just in time.

When he finally walked through the front door, safe and sound, Mother clutched him as if she might never let go.

Much to everyone's relief, he was home. But the world would never be the same again.

The war strained my relationship with Fritz – not just because we inevitably saw less of each other, but because it exposed the gulf between our perspectives.

He had been assigned to a Signal Corps unit in Calw, west of Stuttgart, and wrote to me on the third of September, the day Britain and France declared war on Germany. His letter troubled me. He spoke of finally having the chance to put his training into practice, as though this were some kind of adventure. It sounded as if he was *excited*.

I replied two days later, unable to hide my dismay. I told him I simply couldn't comprehend a world in which people were constantly in danger from other people. It was appalling. 'Don't say it is for the Fatherland,' I wrote. That was what *everyone* was saying. Instead, I reminded him of the summer – of golden sand and the sea spray on our faces at Heiligenhafen. The warmth of those days already felt like a distant memory.

That September, the schools did not reopen, and no one knew when they would. With Hans still in Ulm, waiting to return to Munich, we spent our time sketching the old houses on Münsterplatz or swimming in the Iller while the weather remained warm enough. Life continued much as before, though rationing forced us to cut back here and there. I tried to hold on to the things that brought me joy – the flowers in the garden, music, art. But when I wrote to Fritz about such things, I wondered if they meant anything to him anymore. Still, I pressed a cornflower into an envelope, sent him a four-leaf clover, tucked in a few photographs from Easter. I wanted him to remember that the world held more than war.

People around us seemed confident that Hitler would blockade Britain into submission and that the war would be over quickly. I didn't believe that. Something deep inside me told me this war would last a long time.

Fritz, meanwhile, was frustrated. The French had not stormed across the Rhine as some had expected, and instead of heading to the front lines, he found himself stuck with a desk job – drafting departmental orders, discussing communication strategies. It didn't satisfy him. He would much rather, he admitted, be stationed with an infantry regiment or flying with the Luftwaffe. That admission horrified me. I made my stance clear: I wanted nothing to do with war, or with the shedding of blood.

My words unsettled him. He confessed that I had 'stirred up an internal controversy.' Two years ago he had believed he understood war, that his path had been clear. But now, he felt like a child, only just beginning to learn.

I was planting seeds of doubt, and that gave me hope.

But then his next words undid me. He told me he 'could not take my side' – not because he disagreed with me, but because he lacked the courage to follow that path to its conclusion.

That saddened me, but I wasn't ready to give up on him.

By the end of September, Hans returned to Munich and, at last, my school reopened. But no one talked about the war, even though it must have been on everyone's mind. People have an astonishing ability to shut out what is too unbearable to face. In Ulm, war was still something distant, something abstract.

I wanted to get some photographs developed to send to Fritz, but the photographers were overwhelmed with war work, and the wait was longer than usual. I continued to write to him, clinging to the memories of our time by the North Sea.

Do you remember how I fell asleep on your shoulder on the bus from Heiligenhafen to Kiel?

I reminded him of the little things, the ordinary moments that had once been ours.

But uncertainty gnawed at me.

Fritz had been transferred to work in a prison, and I couldn't help myself – I asked whether he now came into contact with women. Anxiety must have been weighing on me, because around that time, I had a disturbing dream. I dreamt that I was locked in a prison cell for the duration of the war, an iron ring tight around my throat.

I believe dreams reflect the things we do not say aloud. The war, the separation, my fear of losing Fritz – it was all there, in that cold, oppressive cell of my imagination.

I longed for another trip together, just the two of us, somewhere private where we wouldn't be disturbed. But only for a few days – because I also feared the idea of being too closely tied to someone. I wanted love, but I also wanted my freedom.

Music and poetry helped keep my mood up. I sang Schubert songs with Inge, and Werner's violin playing was improving all the time. As the year drew to a close, I took comfort in the familiar rituals of Advent – lighting the candles, singing carols. I made an Advent wreath for Fritz with little red candles and reminded him when to light them. I sent him apples, chocolates, a precious beeswax candle. Small tokens of warmth in an ever-darkening world.

Hans came home from Munich for Christmas, and my joy at seeing him was immense. The winter that year was hard and bitterly cold, but that didn't stop the two of us from taking long walks in the snow-covered woods, the freezing mist obscuring the trees ahead. We dared each other to test the ice on the Iller, laughing breathlessly when we made it to the other side without falling through.

We must have thought we were invincible.

Chapter Eleven

February 1943

I wake to the sound of boots pounding the corridor. The machine that is Gestapo HQ starts early. Keeping eyes on an entire population must be exhausting work.

Else is already up and dressed, her face set in its usual mask of quiet endurance. Though she is a prisoner, she is forced to work in administration for the Gestapo. She keeps her head down, follows orders, and survives. I don't know how she does it – spending her days among the very people she despises.

We share a meagre breakfast of dry bread and lukewarm, tasteless coffee. I think of the samovar in our apartment in Munich, the way Hans and I would use it to make tea. He brought it back from Russia last year when he was stationed there. The memory makes my stomach clench. I force down the bread to keep my strength up and swallow the coffee, bitter and thin, to keep myself alert.

'Stay strong,' Else whispers as the guards arrive to take me to the first interrogation of the day.

I am led back to Mohr's office. He is seated behind his large desk, looking more severe than usual. The stenographer is ready at her machine, her fingers poised, her face expressionless. I lower myself into the chair opposite Mohr, straightening my spine, willing myself to appear unshaken.

He eyes me coldly, then lights a cigarette, blowing a slow stream of smoke into the air. Through the window, I catch a glimpse of blue sky. The world outside still exists – ordinary people walking, laughing, carrying on as if everything is normal. Do they know what is happening behind these walls? I think of my family. I ache to see Hans, even for a moment. What harm could it do now?

Mohr reaches into a file and pulls out a piece of paper. A leaflet. One of ours.

'This,' he says, flapping the paper towards me, 'was handed in to us by a *diligent* member of the public.'

Of course it was. We knew some leaflets would end up in Gestapo hands. Possessing such literature is a crime. And in this climate of fear, people are eager to prove their loyalty – turning in their neighbours, even their own families.

Mohr's eyes bore into me. 'It is entitled *Pamphlets of the White Rose*.' He pauses, then reads aloud: "'We will not be silent. We are your bad conscience."' He looks up, his gaze sharp. 'Who are "we"? What is this "White Rose"?'

I hesitate. The core of our movement is small – Hans, Alex Schmorell, Willi Graf, Christoph Probst, Traute Lafrenz, and me. And, of course, Professor Huber, the author of the latest leaflet, the one we were caught distributing. But beyond us, there is a wider network – supporters who help us financially, or who carry our leaflets to other cities. How much does Mohr already know?

He repeats the question, more forcefully this time. 'Who are the White Rose?'

I meet his stare. 'It refers to my brother and me.'

His eyebrows lift in mock amusement. "Just the two of you?"

I nod.

He scoffs. 'So why give yourselves a name? To sound more important than you are?'

I shrug. 'People take ideas more seriously if they think they come from an organised group.'

Mohr lets out a harsh, dry laugh. 'And yet,' he says, picking up another leaflet, 'this one is titled *Leaflets of the Resistance Movement in Germany*. That doesn't sound like *just* you and your brother.'

'It was still only the two of us.'

Mohr leans back in his chair, studying me. Then he flicks through his file and pulls out another document. 'What about your brother's friends? Alexander Schmorell. Willi Graf. Christoph Probst.'

I flinch before I can stop myself.

He's done his homework.

'Did they also go to Eickemeyer's studio?'

I choose my words carefully. 'They may have. When we showed Eickemeyer's pictures to our friends.'

Mohr smirks. He knows I am playing for time. 'And what about Christoph Probst?' His tone is casual, but I hear the trap closing. 'Did he distribute leaflets in Salzburg and Linz? It would have been easy for him – after all, he's based in Innsbruck with the Luftwaffe.'

'No.' I shake my head emphatically. 'We never asked him to do that. Not with a wife and three children.'

Mohr slams his hand on the desk. 'And yet *he wrote a draft of another leaflet*! So he must have been involved. Enough of this game. It's time you started giving me *names*.'

'No one else was involved,' I say firmly. 'Just Hans and me.'

My heart is hammering. How much longer can I keep this up?

Mohr exhales sharply, shoving his chair back. He strides to the window, staring out, frustrated. The stenographer pauses, hands hovering over the machine. A rare silence settles over the room.

I take a slow, steadying breath.

Mohr lights another cigarette, takes a drag, then turns back to me. His weariness is evident now. He returns to his desk, pulls open a drawer, and takes out another notebook. An involuntary shiver runs down my spine.

I *know* that notebook.

It's the one I used to keep track of our expenses.

Mohr flips through the pages, running a finger down an entry. 'According to these records, in January you purchased *ten thousand sheets of paper* and *two thousand envelopes*.' He pauses, glancing up. 'A staggering amount of stationery, wouldn't you say?'

'My brother and I did that.'

Mohr leans forward. 'Where did you get the money?'

'My father gives me 150 Reichsmarks a month,' I say. 'Hans receives a salary from the military.'

Mohr snorts. 'That's barely enough to live on, let alone fund a mass printing operation.' He taps the notebook. 'So where did the *rest* come from?'

I hesitate. The truth is obvious, but saying it out loud feels dangerous.

'We borrowed from our friends,' I admit.

Mohr's eyes glint with triumph. 'And what did these *friends* think they were funding?'

'I don't know,' I say. 'We made excuses.'

'Don't lie to me!' His voice lashes through the air, and he slams the notebook shut. 'Do you expect me to believe these people handed over money without *asking* what it was for?' He leans back, crossing

his arms. 'We have their names. We *know* your brother served on the Eastern Front with Willi Graf and Alexander Schmorell. They saw war firsthand. They talked about it, didn't they?'

I meet his gaze. 'Yes. They were medics. They saw what was happening.' My voice is steady. 'Of course they talked about it. But no one dares speak openly. People are afraid.'

Mohr nods. 'Afraid. And yet some people *aren't* afraid, are they?' He picks up another document. 'People who paint slogans on public buildings. *Down with Hitler! Freedom!*' He studies me. 'Was that also your work?'

I swallow hard. I had nothing to do with the graffiti. That was Hans and Alex. But I cannot let them take all the blame.

'Yes,' I say. 'Hans and I.'

Mohr shakes his head. 'So let me get this straight. You and your brother – just the two of you – wrote and distributed thousands of leaflets *alone*. And in your spare time, you painted treasonous slogans across Munich, *while also managing to study, travel, eat, and sleep*?' His lips curl. 'I *congratulate* you on your efficiency.' He leans forward. 'Germany needs people like you. You just need to be re-educated.'

I remain silent.

He stubs out his cigarette, then beckons the stenographer. She brings a typed sheet. Mohr slides it across the desk. 'Here is your confession.' He offers me his pen.

I hesitate. My hands tremble as I pick up the paper. The words blur for a moment. Signing this means the loss of my freedom. Perhaps my life.

But if I die, can others be saved?

I pick up the pen. And sign.

Chapter Twelve

1940

The year did not get off to a promising start. My friend Susanne Hirzel and I received official notification that we would be drafted into the Reich Labour Service as soon as we had passed our *Abitur* exams. Though we had drifted apart after our time in the League of German Girls, this unwelcome news rekindled our friendship, uniting us in mutual indignation.

I wanted to join Hans in Munich. Susanne, a talented cellist, hoped to study music in Stuttgart. Neither of us wanted the state dictating our futures.

'The Nazis think women who want to study need to experience manual labour the most,' Susanne grumbled one afternoon as we walked along the icy banks of the Danube.

'We have to find a way out of this,' I said, my stomach knotting at the thought of six months of backbreaking work, crammed into dormitories, and subjected to nightly lectures on National Socialism.

But uncertainty hung over us. We didn't even know *when* our final exams would take place because the Education Minister kept postponing the announcement. I wrote to Fritz, venting my frustration. The waiting felt like torture.

I understand these concerns might seem trivial in the midst of a war. But what eighteen-year-old doesn't put themselves first? What student on the brink of graduation doesn't dream about their future? The war had not yet touched us directly. Our little world still felt intact.

To distract myself, I focused on something far more exciting – planning a ski trip with Fritz. He had missed Christmas in Ulm, so I longed for us to make up for lost time together in the mountains. We debated whether to take a short weekend break or an extended trip, but his movements were unpredictable. He had been stationed in Düsseldorf for a time, and his letters often arrived late due to postal delays.

'Let's go as soon as the *Abitur* is over,' he wrote. 'The war is escalating. I might not get another chance.'

Of course, that depended on whether the *Abitur* would even take place.

In the end, Fritz was granted leave in early March, and we managed to steal four days together in between my exams. We hadn't seen each other for three months, and when I finally laid eyes on him, I felt an overwhelming rush of happiness.

We travelled to the Alps near the Austrian border, and *oh*, it was glorious! The sun shone brightly, making the snow sparkle like crushed diamonds. It was so warm I skied in my swimsuit, basking in the feel of the sun on my skin. By evening, the mountain peaks turned a soft, glowing pink – too beautiful for words. At night, we stood beneath a sky bursting with stars, tracing constellations like secret messages written just for us.

We dined on hearty meals and, afterwards, lay in each other's arms, whispering about the future. I felt as if I had fallen straight from heaven into his embrace.

But all too soon, reality intruded. Fritz had to return to his regiment – this time in Gelsenkirchen, north of Essen, where he complained of drowning in paperwork and coal dust. And I had to return home for the final stretch of my exams.

All we had to sustain us were our memories – the dazzling snow, the scent of pine in the crisp air, moonlit nights – captured in letters we sent back and forth.

Despite the school principal's warnings that I had the 'wrong attitude,' I passed the *Abitur* easily. I was more interested in knowing when Fritz would be back so we could pick up where we had left off. But before I could leave school behind completely, Mother insisted I attend the school-leaving ceremonies on the twentieth of March.

As soon as April arrived, I seized the chance for adventure. Lisa Remppis and I set off on a bicycle tour along the Danube, stopping at the monasteries of Untermarchtal, Obermarchtal, and Zwiefalten. The weather was unseasonably warm, the kind that makes you believe summer has arrived early. We stayed in charming guesthouses and dined magnificently on potato salad, liver dumplings, cake, and ice cream! In the evenings, we strolled by the river, gazing up at the vast sky.

Looking back, my ski trip with Fritz and my bicycle tour with Lisa feel like blissful interludes before the weight of 'duty to the Reich' pressed down on me.

Susanne and I thought we had found a loophole to escape manual labour: enrolling in kindergarten teacher training at the *Fröbel Seminar* in Ulm, the same programme Liesl had completed. Instead of working in fields or factories, we would be caring for children. It was, we convinced ourselves, the perfect solution.

While waiting for our training to begin, I spent my days helping Father finalise his accounts, reading, and cycling whenever the weather allowed. At the *Fröbel Seminar*, we split our time between classroom instruction and hands-on teaching experience. I enjoyed watching the children play, listening to their chatter, their laughter. Our teacher, Fräulein Kretschmer, wasn't a committed Nazi, which made things easier.

But the world outside our little bubble was changing fast.

In April, Germany invaded Denmark and Norway. Fritz was still in Gelsenkirchen, and I missed him desperately. The war, which had once felt distant, now loomed over everything. Some days, I was filled with dread. Other days, I clung to hope. We had been raised to think politically, but now, politics was swallowing our lives. It would have been easier to ignore it – to retreat into art and music – but how could I, when everything around me was being tainted by the same evil?

I poured my emotions into a letter to Fritz. 'Send me your love,' I wrote.

His reply was filled with longing. He wished he could hold me, stroke my hair, make me forget everything. 'I don't fear responsibility,' he confessed. 'But sometimes I feel as if I'm being pushed down a path that isn't my own.'

If he weren't so far away, I would have sent him flowers – anemones, butterfly orchids, violets. But they would have wilted before they reached him. Instead, I told him to pick his own.

I worried about what war would do to him. 'Don't let it make you cruel,' I urged. 'You need a tough mind and a tender heart to stay on the right path.'

As a person and a soldier, Fritz was loyal to a fault, but I could not reconcile myself to the notion that a soldier was obliged to serve his country under any and all circumstances. I thought it would be much better in a war if people could choose the side they believed to be the most just. And it was never justified for a strong country to destroy a weaker one.

Fritz visited Ulm briefly for my nineteenth birthday on the ninth of May. But our time together was painfully short – he had to return to barracks that evening. He was about to be sent into action.

The next day, on the tenth of May, Germany invaded Holland. Fritz wrote from the front lines. He described bombed bridges, burnt houses, overturned cars, dead horses strewn across the streets.

To distract him from the horrors of war, I wrote back about lying in a meadow, beneath a beech tree draped in spider webs that shimmered in the morning light. The meadow by the stream was filled with red carnations and large, juicy marigolds. A bird sang in the tree and another answered from the forest with the same golden melody. War had no place in a world so full of beauty.

Still, I feared that the war was pulling us in different directions. He was trapped in a soldier's life, and I – desperate for something *more* – couldn't pretend to support it.

By mid-May, Fritz was in Belgium. He witnessed a farmer being blown up when he crossed a mined bridge. The man was killed instantly, his body torn apart, limbs flung into the nearby field. Worse still was when the farmer's wife arrived moments later, confused, searching for her husband.

For the first time, Fritz understood the true horror of war.

Later, he listened to a Mozart Minuet on the radio and wrote to me, 'We all listen to Mozart. And yet we still kill each other.'

That, I thought, was the real tragedy.

By the end of June, Fritz was in France, swallowed up by the relentless tide of war. And now, he wasn't the only one I loved who was caught in the conflict. In Munich, Hans had been drafted into the army medical corps. He despised the wasted hours in barracks, the monotony, the waiting, but there was nothing he could do about it. They were kitted out, prepared to be sent to the front.

At first, his unit was stationed in Bad Sooden, and he was able to continue his medical studies in Göttingen. He adored the picturesque town, with its half-timbered houses and peaceful riverbanks. He lodged with an elderly aristocratic lady and, in the evenings, read books or wandered down to the water's edge to talk with the fishermen. It was an idyllic interlude that could never last.

Soon, he too was sent to France, where he worked as a motorbike dispatch rider in Neufchâteau. The bumpy roads left him with swollen wrists, and he crashed more than once, cracking his ribs in the process. But Hans, being Hans, dismissed his injuries as nothing. What really troubled him was the war itself.

Despite being an occupying soldier, he befriended local farmers, practising his French on them, treating them with kindness. I like to think that, in some small way, he showed them that not all Germans were monsters, even though we had invaded their country.

Hans's letters came sporadically, and we clung to any news of his whereabouts. When he did write, he told us that his unit had moved on to Saint-Quentin, where the Germans had seized the finest houses for their own use. It made him deeply uncomfortable. He would have preferred to sleep on straw in a barn than steal someone else's home. Looting was commonplace, and he was appalled by the greed he witnessed.

But nothing compared to what he saw in the field hospitals. The butchery of war sickened him.

After the Franco-German armistice was signed in June, his unit took over a hospital from the Prussians. It held four hundred wounded men, all in desperate conditions. Hans worked tirelessly alongside the French nurses, assisting with twenty operations a day, including amputations. He was learning so much, but at what cost? He began to feel himself growing numb.

In a letter to Inge, he confessed:

> *You may believe a man should return from war wiser and more mature. That only applies in the rarest instance. I was more sensitive before this madness started...We leave the operating theatre with someone dying inside and smoke a cigarette.*

When Paris fell, Fritz wrote to me, hoping that the war would soon be over so we could be together again. But his letters had taken on a different tone – one of quiet disillusionment. He began questioning the senseless destruction, wondering whether humanity lost more in war than it ever gained.

One day, he wrote of burying a French soldier they had found dead in a house in Cambrai. They laid him to rest beside another fallen comrade, beneath a cross inscribed with the words *Pour la France*. 'What does the idea of *La France* truly mean?' he asked me. 'What does *Germany* mean?'

They were weighty questions. And I didn't know how to answer them.

Yet, I too was plagued with questions. My letters to Fritz became darker, more intense, full of thoughts I could no longer keep to myself.

I must have come across as opinionated, but I couldn't understand how so many people remained indifferent.

Ambivalence was everywhere. People cared only for the safe return of their husbands and sons, not for the war itself, or what it meant. And as for the French, I told Fritz I would have admired them more if they had defended Paris to the bitter end instead of worrying so much about their art treasures. Honour, it seemed, was a thing of the past. The only thing that mattered was survival. And saving the Mona Lisa.

Still, I couldn't shake off Fritz's question about nationhood.

The way I saw it, a soldier's duty to his country was like a son's duty to his father. A son promises loyalty – he vows to defend his family in any and every circumstance. But what if that father wrongs another family? Must the son still stand by him?

I knew where I stood. Justice, for me, always took precedence over blind loyalty. Because emotions could lead you astray. And war was the ultimate proof of that.

As part of my kindergarten training, I was required to complete a four-week placement at a children's sanatorium in Bad Dürrheim, a small spa town nestled in the Black Forest. In August, I arrived at the private establishment run by Major Kohlermann and his wife, a rambling old house on the outskirts of town, edged by dense woodland.

The children ranged from toddlers to teenagers – some as young as three, others nearly grown at seventeen. All came from privileged families who could afford the exorbitant fees. But wealth had not shielded them from suffering. Many were asthmatic, and the Kohlermanns believed that breathing difficulties were often tied to psychological distress. Their approach combined medical care with an abundance of warmth and affection. The *Aunties*, as we carers were called, were encouraged to hug the children, to hold them, to provide the closeness and security they needed. With the little ones, this came naturally. The older ones, of course, needed a different kind of support – gentler, more measured, but no less vital.

The setting was idyllic, and the ethos of the Kohlermanns admirable. The children's artwork covered the walls, making the sanatorium feel more like a home than a medical institution. But the work itself was relentless. Caring for small children is exhausting. Every night, I washed five of them from head to toe, dressed them, comforted those who woke crying in the dark, and dealt with the inevitable bed-wetting. There were times when I wondered how I would survive the sheer physical and emotional demands. But the joy of caring for these helpless little creatures sustained me. Without that, I don't know how I would have coped.

If the children were a source of warmth, my assigned roommate was quite the opposite. She devoured trashy romance novels, snored like a train, and seemed to have an aversion to soap and water. I ignored her as best I could.

Whenever I found a quiet moment, I wrote to Fritz. Looking back, I must have bored him senseless with my descriptions of meal schedules and supervising the older children as they clipped their nails and scrubbed behind their ears. But these were the rhythms of my life at the sanatorium – monotonous, repetitive, all-consuming. Fritz, meanwhile, was still in France, where his days were hardly more interesting than mine. We were both living off memories of last summer's holiday by the North Sea, but those golden days were slipping further into the past. Now that France had fallen, we expected Hitler to turn his sights on England at any moment.

Receiving Fritz's letters was the highlight of my days. But one letter, in particular, sent me into a storm of epistolary fury.

The tension between us had always simmered beneath the surface – his choice of career was a constant point of contention – but now he had written something that enraged me beyond measure. He claimed that being a soldier was about 'teaching people to be honest and modest.'

Honest and modest!

I could barely contain myself as I wrote back.

> *Honesty and modesty are the moral duties of every human being, not just soldiers!*

His profession, I argued, was about following orders, nothing more. Where was the virtue in blind obedience? And how could he swear an oath to Germany one moment and then, without hesitation, swear another to Hitler? Was that not a form of deception? Knowing Fritz as I did, I knew he did not truly believe in war – yet there he was, training men to fight in one.

I pushed him further.

> *Shouldn't people fight on the side they believe to be just and right, regardless of their nationality?*

He had no answer to that.

And then, all at once, my four weeks in Bad Dürrheim were over.

To my surprise, I felt a pang of sorrow as I prepared to leave. Somehow, amid the noise and exhaustion, the constant demands and sleepless nights, the sanatorium had become a part of me. Even Frau

Kohlermann, who was strict but wise, had earned my respect. Before I left, she pressed 50 Reichsmarks into my palm – my first ever wages.

I didn't expect to be moved by my departure. But when one little boy clung to me, sobbing inconsolably, my heart broke.

Perhaps, despite everything, I had made a difference.

In September, Hans returned to Munich to resume his studies, and I was back at the Fröbel Seminar in Ulm. Fritz remained in France, stationed on the coast at Wissant near Calais. And so began one of the most difficult phases of our relationship – one that is painful for me to think about even now.

I have always believed in honesty, even when it is uncomfortable. Looking back, I know there was fault and misunderstanding on both sides. I cannot place all the blame on him; I must take my fair share, too.

Perhaps our disagreements about the soldier's life had driven a wedge between us. Fritz had entered the military with honourable intentions – he had always been a man of integrity – but my relentless questioning of war, obedience, and duty must have unsettled him more than I realised.

On the morning of the twenty-sixth of September, a letter arrived for me. I recognised Fritz's scrawl immediately and carried it to the breakfast table, eager to hear from him.

'Is that from Fritz?' Mother asked hopefully as I tore open the envelope.

'Yes.' I pulled out the paper, unfolding it with my usual anticipation.

'How is he?' she pressed, pouring me a cup of tea. She always asked after Fritz and liked exchanging news with his mother, Frau Hartnagel.

I glanced at the first lines. My breath caught. 'He's, er... he's fine.'

'Still in Calais?'

I nodded, suddenly unable to swallow a single bite of breakfast. I needed to be alone to read this letter properly, to absorb what it was saying. Muttering something about needing to get ready for college, I took the letter and retreated to my room.

It was dated a week earlier – war was making the post unbearably slow. I sat on my bed, my fingers gripping the page, my heart hammering as I reread those first few sentences.

Fritz began by saying this was the most difficult letter he had ever written to me. He had debated whether to write it at all, but he had come to the conclusion that I deserved the truth – that I deserved to know who he really was.

I braced myself and read on.

He had been in Amsterdam, sitting alone in a café. The pianist was playing Chopin. (Maybe he thought that detail would soften the blow of what came next.) At the next table sat a young woman, her eyes dark and melancholy, her gaze lingering on him. A Yugoslavian, he found out later. But in that moment, all that mattered were her eyes. She gave him a sad smile, and 'then everything just happened.'

They spent the night together in a hotel.

He spared me the details, but he did not try to justify himself. As he held her in his arms, he wrote, he had been consumed by conflicting thoughts – guilt for betraying me, but also a creeping realisation that our relationship had lost its direction. And yet, when he returned to Calais, he lay awake in bed and cried – not because of what he had done, but because despite everything, *it was still me he wanted.* His love for me had only intensified. It made him happy and unbearably sad at the same time.

He begged for my forgiveness. If he had hurt me, he hoped I could be merciful.

Such a letter demanded a response, but I had no idea what to say.

I wrote back, but only to acknowledge receipt of his letter. I thanked him for his honesty, then filled the page with trivialities – the tailor altering a jacket, my studies, anything that avoided addressing the storm in my heart. I promised to respond properly later, once I had sorted through my thoughts.

But then I added something else.

Don't forget the Yugoslavian woman on my account.

I don't know what I meant by that. Was it meant to be a challenge? A test? Was I trying to appear emotionally detached, to prove to myself that I was above jealousy? Or was I simply trying to protect myself from my own disappointment?

The truth was, I *did* understand. The war and our long separation had placed an impossible strain on us. How could I expect Fritz to resist every temptation, alone for months on end, surrounded by nothing but the monotony of army life? And the woman – what was *she* doing alone in a foreign city in the middle of a war? I could almost pity her.

I pressed Fritz to tell me when he would next get leave. Then I signed off. My head ached. I couldn't write anymore.

Fritz came to Ulm in early October and stayed with his parents. We went for walks along the Danube, trying to reclaim the easy familiarity we had once shared. But he wanted answers, clarity.

I couldn't give them to him.

I *loved* him, but I struggled with the idea of being bound to someone. Solitude was as essential to me as air and water. I needed it, craved it, *protected* it. I wanted Fritz to understand that.

He left Ulm feeling unsettled, and I couldn't blame him.

When Christmas came, Fritz was still stuck in Calais, lamenting the grey skies and damp, miserable air. I, meanwhile, went skiing with my family, grateful for the cold, crisp beauty of the mountains.

Looking back, I know I was emotionally immature. I was too young to navigate something so complicated, too proud to admit how much his letter had shaken me. I wonder if Fritz ever truly forgave me for my indifference.

But it is too late to ask him now.

Chapter Thirteen

February 1943

'Drink.' Mohr pushes a cup of coffee across the desk toward me.

I hesitate. A trick? Poison, perhaps? But then he pours one for himself from the same pot and takes a sip. I inhale the deep, rich aroma – real coffee. None of the cheap *ersatz* substitute that the rest of us have to make do with. Despite my suspicions, the temptation is too strong. I lift the cup to my lips. It is hot, smooth, comforting.

Mohr lights a cigarette, inhales deeply, then exhales. He seems more relaxed today, almost pensive. Perhaps now that I've signed my confession, he no longer sees a need for intimidation. I wonder what this conversation is really about.

'You want the best for the German people, don't you?' he asks, watching me carefully.

'Yes, of course,' I say, and then, instinctively, 'but–'

He lifts a hand to silence me. 'I can see that your methods were... peaceable. Leaflets and slogans. No bombs. No bullets.'

'We believe in the power of words,' I reply. 'We were raised to think for ourselves.'

Mohr pulls a face, as if *thinking for oneself* is a foreign and unpleasant concept. 'You and your brother are intelligent young people. And yet you persist in breaking the law?'

'We don't see it that way.'

'Then how *do* you see it?'

'We follow our consciences.'

'Pah! *Conscience!*' Mohr stubs out his cigarette so hard that the coffee cups rattle. 'What has conscience got to do with anything? The law is what provides order and stability. Without it, there is only chaos.'

'Before the Nazis came to power, the law protected free speech,' I counter. 'Now, it punishes those who dare to speak the truth. No one can say what they really think anymore, because they fear being taken away in the night.'

Mohr's expression tightens. '*The law is the law!* We cannot have everyone deciding for themselves what is right and wrong. Where would that lead? *Democracy?'* He spits the word as if it has a foul taste.

'In a democracy, people would be safe from the whims of a dictator,' I say evenly.

Mohr inhales sharply. 'How dare you deride the *Führer* in that way!' He rises from his chair and paces to the window. I take the opportunity to drink the last of my coffee, feeling the warmth settle in my stomach.

After a moment, he turns back, having composed himself. He smooths his uniform, sits, and steeples his fingers in front of him. 'Fräulein Scholl, you are well-educated. You must see the great benefits National Socialism has brought to Germany. The Treaty of Versailles left our nation on its knees – crippled by inflation, unemployment, poverty.'

I say nothing. I know where this is going.

Mohr leans forward. 'And yet, thanks to *Adolf Hitler*, all that has changed. Inflation has plummeted. Unemployment is gone. Germany is strong once more. The *Führer* has restored our national pride.'

'Hitler has led us into a bloody war,' I reply.

Mohr's face darkens. '*No.*' He shakes his head sharply. '*This* is not a bloody war. It is a *heroic struggle!* We are securing German living space. We are liberating Europe from the Bolshevik threat!'

He *believes* this, I realise. He has swallowed the propaganda whole.

'We are *losing* the war,' I say, my voice steady. 'Our young men are dying by the thousands. We have brought destruction to the countries we occupy. And very soon, Allied troops will march into Germany. The world will condemn us – not only for this war, but for keeping Hitler in power.'

He ignores my talk of defeat. 'And when we *win* the final victory? What will you say then?' His voice drops. 'My own son is fighting on the Eastern Front, doing his duty to the Fatherland.'

There it is. His own son. No wonder he clings so tightly to the fantasy of victory. To acknowledge the truth would mean acknowledging that his own son is being sent to die for a lost cause.

But he isn't ready to face that truth.

'You must see how your actions undermine people's faith in our leadership,' he says. 'This war requires unity. Your leaflets – your words – sow doubt, weaken morale. In the end, they threaten *military power.*'

Undermining faith in National Socialism was exactly what we intended. If we have succeeded, even a little, then we have not fought in vain.

Mohr pinches the bridge of his nose, as if I am exhausting him. When he speaks again, his tone is softer. 'Fräulein Scholl,' he sighs, 'I believe you are misguided, but I do not believe you are beyond redemption.' He leans in slightly. 'You are young. You have your whole life ahead of you. Young people make mistakes. This' – he gestures to the papers on his desk – 'is a mistake. One that we can correct.'

I remain silent.

He studies me carefully. 'Your brother, on the other hand – he is older. He should have known better. You love him, don't you?'

I stiffen.

'It is *natural*,' Mohr continues. 'Filial affection is admirable. Understandable. Perhaps you followed Hans out of loyalty, without truly grasping the consequences of your actions. Shouldn't we put that in the report?'

I see what he is doing. He is offering me an escape – a way to save myself. He is trying to *rescue* me. Because I am a woman. Because I am young. Because in his mind, I cannot *possibly* have made these choices with full awareness. If I play along, if I claim ignorance, I could walk free. But I will not. To betray my beliefs now would be worse than death.

I lift my chin. 'You are mistaken, Herr Mohr.'

He frowns. 'In what way?'

'I was not misled by my brother. I acted of my own free will. I knew what I was doing, and I knew the consequences if I were caught.'

'But surely you *regret* your actions now?'

I meet his gaze, unwavering. 'No. I regret *nothing*. I would do everything exactly the same, all over again. It is *you* who have the wrong world view. Not I.'

A flicker of something – shock? disbelief? – crosses Mohr's face. Then, just as quickly, it is gone.

He sighs heavily, shakes his head, and picks up the phone on his desk. 'We're finished here,' he tells the adjutant. 'Take her back to the cell.'

As the guards move toward me, I watch Mohr carefully. He should be triumphant. He has caught us, broken our network, secured his victory.

But when our eyes meet one last time, I see something else entirely.

He looks disappointed.

Chapter Fourteen

1941

If I had thought that training as a kindergarten teacher would exempt me from manual labour, I was mistaken. I longed to go to university, to immerse myself in books, ideas, and debates. Instead, I was ordered to get my hands dirty – quite literally.

In March 1941, I received the dreaded news: I was to spend six months in the Reich Labour Service, beginning in April.

Susanne Hirzel and I had chosen kindergarten training with the express hope of avoiding the backbreaking drudgery of farm or factory work. It was a calculated decision, and it worked – for Susanne, at least. The Nazi Party permitted her to proceed directly to her music studies in Stuttgart. But I had no such luck. Instead, I was to be sent to a labour camp in Krauchenwies, about eighty kilometres southwest of Ulm.

When I told my family, they braced themselves for an outburst. And yet, to my own surprise, I reacted with quiet acceptance. Complaining would be futile. Any attempt to appeal to the authorities would only reinforce my helplessness. I decided then and there to approach the situation with a stoic detachment, distancing my inner self from my outward circumstances. If I let my anger take hold, I knew it would consume me.

At least I wasn't the only one in the family being conscripted into servitude. My younger brother, Werner, had barely completed his *Abitur* when he was sent to Brittany to help construct the Atlantic Wall in preparation for a British invasion. He left just days before my own departure. We were being scattered across the Reich like chess pieces, assigned roles in Hitler's grand strategy.

Meanwhile, Fritz was also on the move. He had been transferred to Münster, where he was promoted to Commanding Officer and tasked with forming a new division from scratch. He wrote to me about the immense pressure he was under. His orders were to recruit and train two hundred and fifty men. I could tell from his letters that the burden weighed on him. Fritz was not a man who sought power or thrived on authority. His natural modesty made him an unlikely candidate for such a prominent leadership role.

It was clear he wouldn't be granted leave any time soon. I thought of travelling to Münster to see him, but I only had three free days before reporting to Krauchenwies, and most of that time would have been swallowed up by the train journey. I tried to convince myself that waiting a little longer to see him wouldn't make much difference.

Through sheer perseverance, Fritz managed to complete his assignment, shaping a regiment from nothing. And then, just as he settled into his role, the army abruptly appointed an older Captain to take over command of the recruits. Fritz was demoted back to the position of adjutant – an apparent humiliation. But in his next letter, he admitted to feeling a quiet relief. He had more time for himself now. More time to think. More time to write to me.

And yet, the reprieve wouldn't last. Any day now, he expected to be sent to the Balkans. He had always wanted to see Yugoslavia. But not like this.

I left for the camp at Krauchenwies on Sunday the sixth of April – the same day Germany invaded Greece. Hitler's war machine was grinding through Europe with relentless force, swallowing nations one by one. There was no telling which country would be next.

Krauchenwies was a lesson in hardship. We were eighty girls, crammed into a draughty old castle overrun with mice. My roommates shrieked and scurried onto their beds whenever one darted across the floor, but I found the little creatures rather charming. The cold, however, was another matter. The showers were icy, and our thin blankets did little to keep out the night chill. But I refused to be unclean, so I forced myself to adjust, gritting my teeth as the freezing water ran down my back.

The food was abysmal – watery soup, dry bread, barely enough to sustain us through the long days of fieldwork. But the worst part? Sharing a dormitory with nine other girls. There was no privacy, no solitude. Just the constant noise of whispered gossip, giggles, and the rustling of love letters being reread under the covers by torchlight.

Most of my roommates were enthusiastic followers of the Führer, raised on National Socialist doctrine and wholly incapable of questioning it. They were thrilled when Greece surrendered, mistaking conquest for glory. In the evenings, they gushed over photographs of their boyfriends and brothers in Hitler Youth uniforms, debating which Nazi official was the most handsome, the most heroic. The absurdity of it made me want to scream.

I kept my distance, which earned me the reputation of being aloof. Occasionally, I forced myself to join in their chatter – an experiment in blending in – but afterward, I hated myself for the dishonesty. That wasn't who I was.

Books from home were strictly forbidden, but I had smuggled in a copy of *St. Augustine's Confessions*. I read in bed while the others chattered about boys. I was seeking reassurance that there was a divine order to the world despite the madness engulfing Europe. My roommates mocked me for my choice of reading. They preferred scandalous romances – if they read at all. But I wasn't looking for fleeting amusement. I was searching for meaning. And I found comfort in Augustine's belief that our hearts would only find peace in God.

Our daily labour took us into the fields, where we helped farmers' wives struggling in the absence of their husbands, all of whom had been sent to war. At first, I loathed the mind-numbing drudgery of weeding, especially the backbreaking effort of hoeing turnip fields. Why hadn't someone invented a machine to do this work? But as spring deepened into summer and the crops swayed golden under the sun, I began to find solace in the rhythm of it. The walk through the woods to the farm became something I looked forward to – an escape from the suffocating walls of the castle. And there was something oddly satisfying about clearing a stretch of land, knowing that it was necessary, that no matter what happened in the world, weeds would always grow, and people would always need to pull them up.

At the end of each day, I returned to the castle with aching limbs but a sense of peace.

And in that bleak place, I made an unexpected friend.

Gisela Schertling was unlike the others. She wanted to study art and art history in Munich, and I promised to introduce her to Hans once I finally got to university. She was tall and blonde, whereas I was dark-haired and of average height, but the contrast between us ran deeper than appearances. She had grown up in a National Socialist household, believing she could reconcile being both a good Nazi and a good Christian. Yet she was intelligent and open-minded, willing to discuss politics instead of parroting slogans.

Despite our differences, I liked her down-to-earth manner, and together we found small acts of rebellion. On Sundays, we slipped out early and attended Mass at the Catholic church in town. The flickering candlelight, the scent of incense curling through the air, the hushed reverence of the congregation – all of it stirred something in me. When the service was over, we hurried back to the castle and crawled into bed before anyone noticed we were gone.

Some evenings, we escaped again, sneaking into the church to play duets on the organ – Handel, Bach. The music filled the empty space, lifting our spirits above the grim reality of our days.

In a world growing darker by the day, we clung to these stolen moments of light.

I missed my family terribly at the camp, so I was counting down the days to Sunday, twenty-second of June, when Inge and Werner's friend Otl Aicher were due to visit. I had imagined a carefree afternoon – picnicking in the sunshine, catching up on gossip, finding a brief escape from the dull monotony of Krauchenwies. But before they even arrived, the news shattered any hope of happiness.

Germany had invaded the Soviet Union.

First Poland, then Norway and Denmark, then the Netherlands, Belgium, and France. Then Greece. And now, Hitler had turned his armies toward Moscow. The non-aggression pact with Stalin – signed just two years earlier – had been nothing more than a temporary convenience, a lie told to buy time. The Eastern Front would be a slaughterhouse. The war had already stolen so much, but this would take everything.

I sat stiffly in the grass, my appetite gone, the basket of food between us untouched. Otl, usually so full of sharp observations, was unusually quiet. Inge, ever the practical one, tried to keep the conversation light, but there was no escaping the shadow that had fallen over the day. We knew what this invasion meant. More death, more destruction. The war was no longer contained to distant places. It would reach into every life.

Fritz had been writing less frequently. I told myself it was because he was moving around so much. At the start of the Russian campaign, there was a ten-day postal embargo. I clung to what little news I had. After returning from the Balkans, he had spent eight days in Berlin reporting on his experiences in Yugoslavia. Then he had returned briefly to Münster. And now, he was somewhere in the East.

A letter finally reached me in July, postmarked from Minsk, in Belarus. His words unsettled me.

The German radio stations declared victory after victory – Minsk had fallen, then Smolensk. My dormitory roommates cheered each new announcement, as if they had personally conquered these cities. But Fritz's letters told a different story.

The roads were clogged, the advance agonisingly slow. This wasn't Yugoslavia. Here, they faced real fighting. He barely managed two hours of sleep a night. The officers kept repeating that the war in

Russia would be over in weeks, but Fritz knew better. The Russians weren't going to collapse like the French. They would fight with everything they had.

And the people – he wrote of the faces he saw, lined with exhaustion, worn down with pain and sorrow. The Germans claimed to have 'liberated' them from Bolshevism, but what did that matter? Oppression was oppression, no matter who was in charge – whether the Tsar, Stalin, or Hitler.

With each letter, the war pushed Fritz farther from me, not only in distance but in something deeper, more unspoken. I feared for his safety, but I feared even more for what he was being asked to do.

Four months into my stint at Krauchenwies, I received yet another blow. Women who wanted to study at university would now be required to complete an additional six months of labour service for the Reich. I could have screamed.

I wrote to Hans in utter despair, joking – though not really – that I would gladly contract any reasonably tolerable disease if it meant escaping this fate. That's how desperate I was becoming. I vented to my friend Lisa Remppis, railing against the injustice of being alive during such a momentous, cursed time. But even as I wrote the words, I knew they were nonsense. Perhaps we were actually being given an opportunity to take direct action against the regime. But how? I had no idea. It felt as if we were simply being told to put our lives on hold, to wait – indefinitely. And my patience was wearing dangerously thin.

For a brief period, I was assigned a new job, working for a family in the village. Herr Krele was employed at a munitions factory, and

his wife worked their small farm. I was responsible for their baby
– washing, changing, and feeding him – before tackling the endless household chores. At midday, the mother and their ten-year-old
daughter returned for lunch, and I served them before plunging back
into my routine: washing up, darning, caring for the baby.

Despite the monotony, there were small joys. Summer melted into
autumn, painting the distant woods in a soft blue haze. Mornings were
crisp, the fields glistening with hoarfrost before the sun burned it away.
The quiet rhythm of domestic life soothed me, if only for a little while.

Then, in September, a letter brought welcome news: Fritz was being transferred from Russia to Weimar. He had been assigned to raise
a company for the German Afrika Korps in Libya. I exhaled in relief.
At least he was out of Russia. The war in the East was dragging on, and
as the German army advanced toward Leningrad and Moscow, winter
set in with its full, merciless force. The Nazis launched a nationwide
campaign urging civilians to donate warm woollen clothing for the
troops at the front.

I refused to donate a single thing.

Even when Fritz wrote to me, describing the brutal conditions –
soldiers without gloves, frostbitten hands, men shivering in their thin
uniforms – I would not waver. What did it matter, I argued, whether
it was German soldiers or Russian soldiers freezing to death? It was
terrible either way. But by now, I had come to a firm conviction: Germany must lose the war. Any act that prolonged it – even something
as simple as donating a pair of socks – was unacceptable to me.

Fritz, of course, didn't see things the way I did. But he never tried
to convince me otherwise. Maybe, deep down, he knew I was right.

In October, I was sent to the War Auxiliary Service Camp in Blumberg, a small town near the Swiss border. My assignment was at the National Socialist kindergarten, caring for children too young to understand the world they had been born into.

Blumberg, nestled among the rolling hills of the Schwarzwald, should have been beautiful. But the reopened iron ore mine scarred the landscape, a gaping wound feeding the war machine. Hitler needed iron, and the mine needed bodies. Thousands of Yugoslav prisoners were transported to Blumberg to work in the mines, forced into barracks that were barely fit for animals, let alone men. Dust and mud coated the streets and buildings. Enormous warehouses loomed, hastily constructed to store iron ore before it was shipped west.

I lodged with the family who ran the local guesthouse, good people in their own way – friendly, warm, generous with their food. They looked after me as if I were their own daughter, and in their comfortable home, I was well-fed and safe. At the kindergarten, I adored the children, playing with them in the sandbox, listening to their laughter. Their small arms wrapped around me in affection.

So why wasn't I happier?

Maybe it was the contrast – the unbearable gulf between my existence and that of the prisoners who laboured in the mines. My host worked as a guard, keeping the Yugoslavs in check. I should have been appalled by this. Perhaps, deep down, I was. But I also needed to feel safe. And so, I forced myself not to dwell on the injustices around me.

I sought answers in the pages of St Augustine, desperate for reassurance that there was order amidst the chaos. At night, I poured my heart out to God in my diary: *Thou hast created us in Thine image.* But had He created us to be this? I prayed for strength, knowing how much weakness there was in me. I felt lost, waiting for some great test that would prove who I truly was.

Even writing to Fritz became difficult. It felt like I had nothing to say. He was stationed in Weimar, at a loose end, waiting for orders. We planned to meet at the end of October in Augsburg, but our long-awaited reunion was a failure from the moment we arrived.

The hotel – a modest, fading place – felt stifling. No sooner had we closed the door than Fritz was all over me, desperate for closeness after so many months apart. But I couldn't respond.

Looking back, I know now that it wasn't about Fritz. It was about everything I was struggling with – the contradictions of my life, working for the National Socialist state, living with a 'good German' family, pretending everything was normal while all around me, the war raged on. The prisoners. The bombings. The death toll climbing ever higher in the East. I needed to feel close to God, and in my confusion, I pushed away everything else. Including Fritz.

He didn't deserve that.

Perhaps he realised that, because as soon as he returned to Weimar, he wrote. He wanted to make things right between us. He suggested we pray together.

I wrote back, of course I did. I couldn't bear to lose him over a single, painful misunderstanding. He meant too much to me. And over the following weeks, we re-established our relationship through letters. Fritz told me that he now understood what it meant to love truly – to give without demanding anything in return.

He expected to be sent to North Africa at any moment. It could be six months before we saw each other again, possibly longer. So he took a risk.

On Sunday, the ninth of November, he defied army regulations and travelled 530 kilometres to Freiburg – well beyond the 100-kilometre Sunday travel limit. He did it for me, to save me the burden of making the longer journey.

We wandered through the medieval streets, our boots echoing on the cobblestones, the air crisp with the scent of autumn leaves and wood smoke. We talked about God, about what it meant to truly love another person. I told him my greatest fear – that I longed to be loved, but that longing itself felt like a weakness.

Fritz took my hands in his, his grip warm against the cold. 'If love comes from God,' he said, 'then longing for the love of another person is also the longing for the love of God.'

He spoke the words as if they were the simplest, most self-evident truth. He saw everything so clearly. He taught me I was worthy of love.

Fritz's expected deployment to North Africa never came. Instead, he travelled from Weimar to Freiburg most weekends in November and December. I would meet him at the station at six on Saturday evening. He would leave again on the Sunday night train.

We had only twenty-four hours together, but little by little, Fritz's patience taught me how to love him again.

On the seventh of December, Japan bombed the U.S. naval base at Pearl Harbor. Four days later, Germany declared war on America. The war had now become truly global, stretching across continents and oceans. How much longer could this madness go on?

I spent Christmas that year back in Ulm. Fritz was still in Weimar. We had hoped to see each other over the holidays, but military obligations kept him away. I longed for his presence, but I had begun to accept that longing was something I would have to live with.

At the New Year, I escaped to the mountains with Hans and Inge for a skiing trip. Hans's girlfriend, Traute, joined us, along with two other friends, Ulla and Wulfried. Outside, storms howled through the valleys, but inside our cabin, we created our own world – one of books, music, and conversation. We read aloud from Dostoevsky, his words lingering in the air like smoke from the fireplace. We sang hymns in the flickering candlelight. And we talked.

Hans was preoccupied, as always, with questions of morality and resistance. He had been deeply moved by the sermons of Bishop Clemens August von Galen of Münster, one of the few voices in Germany daring to speak out against Hitler.

'It sickens me,' Hans said one evening, his voice taut with frustration, 'that the Church remains silent. How can they claim to be followers of Christ and yet accept Hitler without question?'

He had a point. The official Church had largely fallen in line with the Nazi regime, choosing to survive rather than resist. But Bishop Galen was different. He spoke the truth, even at great personal risk.

'People will ask,' Hans continued, his eyes dark with intensity, '*What did you do about this terror?* And what will we say?'

Bishop Galen had been one of the first to publicly denounce the Nazis' euthanasia programme, which had begun as a 'mercy killing' initiative but had rapidly expanded into the systematic murder of the mentally and physically disabled. The programme operated under the guise of eliminating 'life unworthy of life,' a phrase that made my stomach turn.

We had already heard whispers about it ourselves. Mother's friends from her nursing days had spoken in hushed voices of black trucks arriving at a nearby institution for disabled children. The children were taken away. None ever returned.

Bishop Galen had thundered from the pulpit: 'An obedience that enslaves souls is the uttermost slavery.' His words were printed and shared. They resonated with us.

Hans set down his book, his mind already racing ahead. 'You know,' he said, his voice filled with conviction, 'one should definitely have a duplicating machine of one's own.'

A duplicating machine. A way to spread words that could not be spoken aloud. A way to break the silence.

None of us knew it yet, but that evening in the mountains – while the snowstorm raged outside and we sat safe and warm in the flickering candlelight – something had been set in motion. A seed had been planted.

And it would grow.

Chapter Fifteen

February 1943

The guards march me back to the cell where Else is waiting. As soon as the door slams shut behind me, she's at my side.

'Well?' she asks, searching my face. 'What did he want this time?'

I feel utterly drained. The conversation with Mohr has left me hollow, as if I've spent the last hour arguing with a wall, hurling myself against something immovable. 'He offered me a way out,' I say finally. 'He tried to save me.'

Else's face lights up with sudden hope. 'Oh, Sophie, that's wonderful—'

'I turned him down.'

The light in her eyes flickers out. She moves closer, her voice dropping to a whisper. 'But why, Sophie?'

I shake my head. How can I explain? 'He wanted me to say that I had made a mistake. That I was young and misled by Hans. That I didn't really know what I was doing.' I take a deep breath, trying to put into words what I already know in my heart. 'But I *did* know. And if I admitted otherwise, it would mean abandoning everything we stood for. It would mean betraying Hans. Betraying the White Rose.'

Else presses her lips together, then reaches for my hand. 'But, Sophie... you *are* young. You still have your whole life ahead of you. Think about your parents. Your family. Why not accept his offer? If it means you can survive...'

I squeeze her hand gently, then let it go. 'It's too late,' I say, though I'm not sure if I mean that the opportunity has passed or that I was never going to take it in the first place.

Else opens her mouth as if to argue, but before she can say anything, the air raid siren wails through the prison. A cold, mechanical shriek that rattles through the walls and sets my pulse racing.

Else gasps and scrambles under the table. 'Sophie, come away from the window!' she hisses.

But I don't move.

I step forward and press my hands against the cold glass, looking up into the dark sky. In the distance, the low hum of engines swells into a roar. British RAF bombers streak overhead. And then –

A deafening explosion.

A burst of fire blooms in the night, turning the sky red, casting long, flickering shadows against the prison walls. The ground trembles beneath my feet. The air vibrates with the distant rumble of collapsing stone.

Else curls tighter under the table, but I stay where I am.

I am not afraid.

The bombs are not a threat. To me, they are hope.

Hope that the world outside has not forgotten us.

Hope that the sky itself is bearing witness.

Chapter Sixteen

January – May 1942

Before returning to Blumberg in the New Year, I visited Hans in Munich. He was eager to introduce me to someone he held in the highest regard.

Hans had met Dr. Carl Muth the previous summer through their mutual friend, Otl Aicher. Otl had arranged for Hans to deliver a bust of Blaise Pascal to the elderly scholar's home, a task that might have taken only a few minutes but instead turned into an hours-long conversation. Dr. Muth invited Hans inside, and the two immediately bonded over a shared love of books. What started as a chance meeting became something more: an apprenticeship of sorts, with Hans spending countless afternoons cataloguing and arranging Muth's vast and chaotic library.

I should explain that Carl Muth was no ordinary scholar. He was the founder and editor of *Hochland*, a renowned magazine that had once published articles on literature, art, and theology – until the

Nazis banned it for its outspoken criticism of the regime. That alone made him remarkable in my eyes.

So on a crisp January afternoon, Hans and I made our way to the quiet, tree-lined suburb of Solln, where Dr. Muth lived in a charming old house set within a large, wooded garden. Snow clung to the bare branches, and birds flitted between them, undeterred by the cold. There was something peaceful, almost untouched by war, about the place.

If I was charmed by the house, I was utterly enchanted by the man who greeted us at the door. He looked as if he had stepped straight out of the nineteenth century – thin and refined, with a high forehead, an elaborate moustache, and a neatly trimmed goatee. His pince-nez perched on the bridge of his nose, and he wore an old-fashioned wing-collared shirt with a polka-dot cravat. When he saw Hans, his entire face lit up in a dazzling smile.

'Hans, my good fellow.' He shook my brother warmly by the hand. 'How wonderful to see you. And this must be your lovely sister, Sophie.' He took my hand and actually *kissed* it. What a charming gentleman! I fell in love with him there and then. He was so delicate, fragile even, that I wanted to throw my arms around him to stop him fading away.

'Do come in,' said Dr Muth. 'I'll make some coffee.'

Hans took me into the library which also served as Muth's study and living room. Books covered every wall and were piled on the floor in front of the fireplace. His wife had died some years before and he lived alone, surrounded by his many thousands of books.

Dr Muth brought in a tray with coffee and cups. Hans moved some books so there was room to put it down on the desk.

'I apologise for the ersatz coffee,' said Herr Muth, pouring from a pot. 'Dreadful stuff, don't you think?' He passed me a cup.

I took a sip and tried not to grimace. 'It's certainly not the real thing,' I said diplomatically.

We talked about everything that afternoon – poetry, literature, theology, art, music. Dr Muth's knowledge was boundless, like an ocean, but he was just as interested in what *we* had to say. The war, inevitably, entered the conversation.

'The destruction of Cologne,' he said heavily, referring to the bombing by the British, 'is only the beginning. Other cities will suffer the same fate unless this madness is brought to an end.' He sighed and stirred his coffee absentmindedly. 'But that seems unlikely. Rommel presses forward in North Africa, and the Eastern Front pushes deeper into Russia. This war is a machine that will not stop until it consumes us all.'

Hans and I exchanged a glance.

When the conversation turned to Goethe, I mentioned that our father's favourite quote was *Allen Gewalten zum Trotz, sich erhalten.*

'Precisely,' Muth said, his sharp eyes glinting. '*Stand tall against all forces, and survive.*' He leaned forward slightly, his gaze locking onto mine as if he could see straight into my soul. 'And tell me, Sophie, how do you intend to do that?'

His question caught me off guard, but I answered honestly. 'By holding onto what I believe in. Truth, beauty, nature, God.'

Dr Muth studied me for a long moment, then nodded in approval. 'It gives me great joy to know there are young people like you and Hans who will be the custodians of true German values.'

I expected Hans to respond – to agree, to add something – but he was unusually silent. He looked down into his coffee, a small crease between his brows.

Later, I would discover that he had a secret he hadn't yet told me.

After my trip to Munich, I returned to Blumberg, counting down the days until my release from the Reich Labour Service. Life seemed to settle into its familiar rhythm – Fritz remained in Weimar, still awaiting orders to go to North Africa, and Hans continued his studies in Munich. We had all learned to endure, to exist within the confines imposed on us, while quietly dreaming of something more.

And then, without warning, our family was shaken to its core.

Father was arrested by the Gestapo.

It happened just as it had in 1937 – early morning, an unexpected knock at the door, the chill of fear creeping through the apartment in Ulm. It was a Monday in February. Father was getting ready for work, Mother preparing breakfast. Inge had only just returned from visiting Hans in Munich. The doorbell at such an hour could mean only one thing.

The accusation came from someone we had once trusted. Fräulein Wilke, Father's young secretary, had denounced him. She was a devoted Nazi, eager to prove her loyalty to the regime. And Father, with his sharp tongue and unwavering principles, had given her the perfect opportunity.

'If Hitler doesn't end the war soon, the Russians will be in Berlin within two years,' he had remarked at work, voicing the same blunt assessments he made at home. But home was one thing. Saying such things in public – especially in front of someone like Fräulein Wilke – was another matter entirely.

Loyal Nazis had an unshakable belief in Germany's inevitable victory. To them, doubt was treason. And to make matters worse, Father had gone even further. He had called Hitler *a divine scourge*, a punishment upon the people. And then, in the way he always had when debating with Hans back in his Hitler Youth days, he had challenged Fräulein Wilke outright.

'Do you really believe,' he had asked her, 'that this war is being fought for the Fatherland?'

Naturally, she had answered yes.

'On the contrary,' Father had declared, 'this war has nothing to do with the Fatherland. It has everything to do with the Party's hunger for power.'

I can only imagine how those words must have struck her. Was she horrified? Conflicted? Or did she see it as a test of her own devotion?

Perhaps Father had already suspected what was coming. 'So now you can destroy me,' he had added lightly, as if making a joke. 'People are shot for saying things like this.'

Fräulein Wilke did not find it funny.

She went straight to the local Gestapo chief and reported him. Two agents were promptly dispatched.

They took Father into custody that morning.

But for reasons none of us could fully understand, they let him go, pending trial.

Perhaps they considered him too insignificant. Perhaps they were overwhelmed with cases. Or perhaps – most absurdly – Father's arrest had come at an inconvenient time. He was in the middle of preparing the year-end accounts for Ulm's tax office. The bureaucratic machinery of the Reich needed its numbers tallied, and even the Gestapo had to acknowledge that.

But we knew the reprieve was only temporary.

They would come back for him.

And next time, they wouldn't let him go.

In March, Fritz received news that upended his expectations once again. He would not, after all, be going to North Africa with the signal corps unit he had helped create. Instead, he was ordered to go to France with his platoon to rebuild the division, after which he would be deployed to the Soviet Union – a place he had hoped never to see again.

We had only a handful of weekends left together. And after that? There was no telling when – or if – we would see each other again.

Fritz arrived in Freiburg in mid-March, just as I was completing my time with the Reich Labour Service. We clung to those stolen moments, trying to ignore the weight of looming separation. I held on to his voice, his touch, his presence – knowing they would soon be reduced to letters and distant echoes.

By the end of the month, he was in Le Mans after a six-day train journey from Weimar. His first letter from France arrived soon after. He wrote of the spring blossoms outside his window, the golden daffodils swaying in the breeze. For a fleeting moment, their beauty made him happy. But then he remembered why he was there, and everything – the flowers, the sunshine, even the gentle warmth of spring – felt unbearably absurd.

In May, I turned twenty-one and at long last, I had permission to study in Munich.

As the train pulled out of Ulm station, I leaned out of the window, waving to my parents on the platform. Mother's face was a mixture of pride and anxiety. Father stood beside her, hands tucked behind his back, nodding his encouragement. I was to lodge with Dr Muth, at least temporarily, until accommodation could be found for me closer to the city centre.

The train picked up speed, and with each mile that passed, I felt a growing sense of freedom. I had fulfilled my obligations to the Reich Labour Service, done everything the state demanded of me, and now – at last – I could carve out my own path. I was enrolled at the University of Munich to study biology and philosophy. The study of life and the study of how to live. These were the questions that mattered most to me.

The familiar fields of my childhood blurred past the window. A chapter of my life was closing. Ahead lay something new, something unknown. I had insisted on making the journey alone – Mother had offered to accompany me, but I had declined. This was a step I needed to take by myself.

In the luggage rack above me sat my suitcase, a bottle of wine nestled among my clothes. On my lap rested a tin containing the birthday cake Mother had baked for me. I planned to share it with Hans and his friends.

The train rumbled through Augsburg, and soon the western suburbs of Munich came into view. I reached for my suitcase, anticipation quickening my pulse.

When the train slowed at the platform, I clambered down, gripping the cake tin tight. A sea of khaki uniforms surrounded me, filling the station with the sharp scent of wool and leather. I turned, searching the crowd.

'Sophie!'

I knew that voice. I spun around and saw Hans waving at me, pushing through the throng. Relief flooded through me. I dropped my suitcase – though not the cake tin! – and threw my arms around him.

'You made it,' he said, laughing.

He scooped up my suitcase, and together we made our way towards the exit.

'What's in the tin?' he asked.

'A birthday cake. Mother made it yesterday.'

'Excellent,' said Hans. 'We'll eat it tonight when I introduce you to my friends.'

No sooner had Hans met me at the station than he left me in the company of his girlfriend, Traute Lafrenz.

'Come on,' said Traute, picking up my suitcase. 'I'll take you to Dr Muth's house.'

I followed her through the station, trying not to feel annoyed with Hans. He could have arranged his time better. I was grateful for Traute's help, but she seemed distracted, answering my questions in clipped sentences. I wondered if something was wrong between her and Hans, but I didn't press.

We took the tram to Solln, leaving behind the bustle of the city.

Dr Carl Muth welcomed us at the door with his usual charm.

'I've prepared a room upstairs for you, Sophie, dear,' he said. 'I hope you'll be comfortable. And please, help yourself to any books in the library.'

'Thank you, Dr Muth. I'm sure I will be.'

He smiled. 'Of course, a young person like you would rather be in the heart of the city where all the life is. As soon as you find something more suitable, just let me know.'

I was grateful that he understood this was temporary. I hadn't come to Munich to live in a sleepy suburb.

Traute made her excuses and left. I thanked her for her help, then unpacked my clothes, kicked off my shoes, and lay back on the bed, listening to the birdsong outside the open window.

My new life was just beginning.

Hans arrived that evening, full of energy, with no word of apology for abandoning me at the station.

'Settling in all right?' he asked.

'It's fine,' I said. 'Dr Muth is very kind.'

'Super,' said Hans. He wouldn't sit still. 'Come and meet my friends. And bring the cake and wine.'

We took the tram to Athener Platz, where Traute was already waiting.

That night, I met two more of Hans's friends and liked them immediately.

'Alex Schmorell,' said Hans, gesturing towards a lanky young man lounging in an armchair, pipe in hand. 'But everyone calls him Shurik.'

'Hello.' I held out my hand.

He took it and kissed it with exaggerated elegance. 'Delighted to meet you, Sophie.'

'Why do they call you Shurik?' His sharp features and dark, flopping hair gave him a faintly exotic air. I was intrigued.

'My mother was Russian,' he said. 'I was born in the Ural Mountains.' His German had a lilting Russian inflection.

'And he longs to go back,' Hans interjected.

'Most certainly,' said Alex, exhaling a cloud of smoke. 'And I will take my friends with me.'

'And this is Christoph Probst,' said Hans. 'We call him Christel.'

'Does anyone here use their real name?' I laughed, shaking Christoph's hand.

He had light, wavy hair, and there was something easy-going about him, something warm. He reminded me of Hans.

'Now then,' said Hans. 'Sophie's brought a cake because it's her birthday.'

'Then we love her already,' said Alex.

We cut the cake and Hans suggested a game.

'We'll each read a passage of poetry, and everyone else has to guess who wrote it.'

Alex went first. It wasn't hard – everyone knew Heine, Goethe, or Schiller. Then Hans pulled out a typewritten page.

The poem was about a robber who sets out to steal but finds a nation devoid of honour, dulled by spiritual emptiness. The people, desperate for wealth, follow him blindly.

> *Where before one liar raged*
> *Thousands soon were thus engaged.*

It was grim. A world in chaos, overrun by deception. But the ending held hope – one day, the tyrant would fall. It had to be about Nazi Germany, I thought.

'Who wrote it?' Hans asked.

No one knew. We guessed every contemporary poet we could think of.

Alex exhaled another smoke ring. 'We should drop copies from an aeroplane and dedicate it to Hitler.'

Hans's eyes gleamed. 'Great idea, but you still have to guess.'

'You wrote it,' Alex accused.

Hans laughed. 'I wish. No, it was written in 1878 by Gottfried Keller.'

'Keller, the nineteenth-century Swiss poet? You're joking.'

'I'm not. Here – look.' Hans handed over the book.

Christoph shook his head. 'Incredible. It could have been written yesterday.'

'It gives us hope,' Hans said, 'that the tyranny of National Socialism will be overthrown.'

'I'll drink to that!' said Alex.

Suddenly I remembered the bottle of wine. It would now be at an unpalatable room temperature.

'No problem,' said Alex, jumping to his feet. 'It's a beautiful moonlit night. We'll take the wine down to the English Gardens and cool it in the river.'

And so we strolled down to the park which was fresh with spring. Alex brought his balalaika – a stringed Russian instrument similar to a lute – and Hans brought his guitar. We tied a piece of string to the neck of the wine bottle and lowered it into the cool waters of the Isar. We played music and sang songs and shared the cooled wine. It was the best birthday I'd ever had. In that moment, I was happy to be alive.

Hans walked me back to Dr Muth's house at the end of the evening. The streets of Solln were quiet, as if the entire suburb had gone to bed by nine o'clock. The only sounds were the rhythmic tapping of our shoes on the pavement and the distant hum of a tram. I felt pleasantly tired, the evening's warmth lingering in my limbs. Whatever irritation I had felt towards Hans earlier had dissolved. He had been the life of the gathering, lighting up the room with his wit and laughter. But now, as we strolled arm-in-arm, he was uncharacteristically silent.

I glanced at him. His brow was furrowed, his gaze fixed on the cobblestones ahead.

'What are you thinking about?' I asked.

For a moment, he didn't answer. Then he turned to me, his voice quiet but charged with something electric.

'Can you keep a secret, Sophie?'

I stopped walking and faced him. 'You know I can.'

A part of me wondered if he was going to confide something about Traute. They had barely spoken to each other all evening, and I had sensed a coolness between them. If Hans needed relationship advice, I wasn't sure I was the best person to offer it.

But when he spoke again, my stomach tightened.

'I've been talking to Alex and Christoph.' There was something in his tone – serious, urgent – that sent a shiver through me.

'About what?' I asked warily.

Hans exhaled, as if steeling himself. Then, in a voice both soft and resolute, he said, 'Resistance.'

The word cut through the night air like the blade of a knife – sharp, beautiful, dangerous. My pulse quickened. I was suddenly wide awake, more awake than I had felt in weeks.

'What kind of resistance?' My voice was barely above a whisper.

'Remember the sermon we read by Bishop Galen?' His eyes were intent on mine. 'The one denouncing the Nazis?'

'Of course,' I said. The mere memory of it made the hairs on the back of my neck stand up.

'It was copied and distributed.'

I nodded. We had been in awe of the bishop's courage. The words had spread like wildfire despite the regime's efforts to silence dissent.

Hans took a deep breath, as if deciding whether to say what came next. And then, with a rush of words, he did. 'We could do the same, Sophie. Write and distribute leaflets. If people read the truth, if they see through the lies, maybe it will give them the courage to resist.'

We had reached Dr. Muth's house now. I turned to him fully, searching his face in the dim glow of a streetlamp. Was he serious? His eyes burned with excitement, with purpose.

He was serious.

I already knew my answer. It wasn't something I had to deliberate over. It was as if I had been waiting for this moment without even realising it.

'Yes,' I said. 'We'll do it.'

Hans's face broke into a grin – one of triumph, of relief, of something bigger than the two of us.

'But we'll need a duplicating machine,' he said, his mind already racing ahead. 'And those cost a fortune.'

I smiled. An idea was already forming. 'Leave it to me,' I said. 'I'll sort it.'

He looked at me, both grateful and a little in awe. Then he squeezed my hand.

'We're going to make a difference, Sophie,' he said.

And for the first time in a long time, I felt a glimmer of hope.

The next day, Fritz came to see me. He had made time in his busy schedule to travel to Munich. We walked through the English Garden, along the bank of the Isar, enjoying the warm sun on our faces. The trees were coming into leaf and colourful crocuses blanketed the grass.

I should have been paying attention to him – this might have been our last time together before he was sent to the Russian front. But my mind was on the previous night's conversation with Hans.

'Could you get hold of a duplicating machine?' I asked.

Fritz stopped mid-step. 'A what?'

I met his gaze. 'A duplicating machine.'

'Sophie...' He frowned. 'What for?'

I hesitated. If I told him, I would be putting him in danger. 'You could do it through the military,' I ploughed on, ignoring his question. 'Get a requisition order or something. You must use equipment like this all the time.'

'But you still haven't told me what you need it for,' he said patiently.

A small group of us in Ulm including Inge, our friend Otl, and me, liked to write and share stories and poems with friends. We called our little publication *Storm Lantern*. I pretended that the duplicating machine was for that.

'Oh, come off it Sophie,' said Fritz. 'You don't need a duplicating machine for that. Inge can make enough copies with a typewriter and carbon paper. What do you really want it for?'

I sighed. He wasn't going to let it drop. Despite my promise to Hans, I would have to confide in Fritz. I knew I could trust him. 'Hans and I want to print leaflets.'

Fritz's face darkened. He didn't ask what sort of leaflets. He didn't need to. He knew me too well for that. He gripped my upper arms. 'But Sophie, don't you realise this could cost you your head?' There were tears in his eyes.

'I know.'

'And it doesn't bother you?'

'Doesn't it bother you that you might die in Russia?'

He flinched. 'Of course it does! But what choice do I have?'

'And what choice do I have?' I insisted. 'I have to act according to my conscience.'

He hung his head, the fight gone out of him. He must have known he was not going to talk me out of my decision.

'Whatever I think of your plans,' he said, 'I can't do what you're asking. I don't have access to the purchase order stamp. I would have to ask the company sergeant for it and then he would know about the order and it would be traced back to him if...' He trailed off. I think he'd been about to say, 'If everything went wrong.'

'So you can't help me?'

'I'm sorry, Sophie. I can't.' He took out his wallet. 'But I can give you money.' He handed me two hundred Marks. 'Take it. But don't tell me what you're going to do with it.'

'Thank you,' I said, pocketing the money. 'You're too good.'

'And you're too brave,' he said, kissing me on the lips. 'You're the bravest person I know.'

Chapter Seventeen

February 1943

E lse has been away from the cell, doing her job. When she returns, I see from her face that something is wrong.

'What is it?' I ask.

She takes my hand and pulls me away from the door, lowering her voice. 'There's been another arrest.'

My heart slams against my ribs. 'Who?' My first thought is Alex.

'I don't know yet,' Else says. 'But I promise you I'll find out. I have to go.' She returns to her work, leaving me alone.

The wait is agony. I sit on my bunk, my hands clasped in my lap, thinking the worst. It must be Alex. But surely he would have fled Munich as soon as he heard the news of our arrests. He's reckless, yes, but he's also smart. He would have made for the Swiss border the moment he sensed danger. He has the means, the determination. He'd take shelter in a shepherd's hut if he had to. He'd find a way to charm the locals, to blend in. This is what I tell myself, over and over, as if willing it will make it true.

But it's February. The mountains are treacherous at this time of year. Could he survive?

The cell door creaks open. I leap to my feet. Else steps inside, her expression grave.

'Did you find out?'

She moves toward me, her eyes filled with sorrow. 'It's Christoph Probst.'

'No.' The word barely makes it past my lips before my legs give out. I sink onto the bunk, my hands gripping the edge to steady myself. Not Christoph. Not dear, gentle, kind Christoph.

When I thought it might have been Alex, I was afraid – but Alex would have fled. He would not have waited to be arrested. The Gestapo would have a job catching him. But, stuck in Innsbruck, Christoph had no way of knowing what has happened. Besides, Christoph is not a fighter. He is a husband, a father, a man who only ever wanted peace. This should never have happened to him.

I think of his wife. His children. The new baby. The last I heard, his wife was still in the hospital, weak with fever. What will happen to them now?

A sob rises in my throat. Hot tears spill onto my hands. I did not cry when they arrested Hans and me. I did not cry when they locked me in this cell. But I weep now for Christoph.

Else kneels beside me and wraps her arms around me, holding me close. I don't pull away.

Where will this end?

Chapter Eighteen

May – June 1942

At the end of May, Hans moved into a room in Mandlstrasse, just west of the English Garden. I envied him. It was a dream location, in the heart of Munich. Meanwhile, I was still in Solln with Dr Muth, making the long tram journey into the city every day. I don't want to sound ungrateful – I adored Dr Muth – but I longed to be closer to university life, to the pulse of Munich itself.

Dr Muth, ever generous, introduced Hans and me to a fascinating circle of people. There was Sigismund von Radecki, a writer and critic who had converted to Catholicism and translated Russian and English works into German. His satirical essays were as sharp as his wit. Then there was Josef Furtmaier, a former communist and fierce Nazi opponent, whom I privately nicknamed *The Philosopher* – not just because of his ideas, but because he could pontificate for hours without pause. Listening to him and Hans debate left me utterly exhausted.

In truth, I was growing frustrated. All we ever seemed to do was talk. Hans and Alex were still discussing their plan to produce anti-Nazi leaflets, but weeks passed, and nothing materialised. I wanted action, not endless deliberation.

The war weighed heavily on me. With the arrival of warmer weather, the German Army continued its relentless push into Russia. The horror of it all felt never-ending.

I tried to push my anxiety aside and focus on my studies. After all, that was why I had come to Munich. I wanted to make up for the time lost in the Reich Labour Service – time spent hoeing turnips and training to be a kindergarten teacher.

My favourite lecturer by far was Professor Kurt Huber. He taught philosophy in the grand Auditorium Maximum, the university's largest lecture hall. Even with its size, you had to arrive early to secure a seat, his lectures were so popular.

At first glance, he was entirely unremarkable. A man in his late forties, of average height, with greying hair and a perpetually tired expression. His posture was slightly hunched, his suit always a little crumpled. When he walked, his right leg dragged behind him, the lasting consequence of a childhood battle with acute diphtheria. The infection had nearly killed him – doctors had been forced to slit his larynx to save his life. Because of that, his voice often faltered at the beginning of his lectures, and his hands had a tendency to tremble.

None of that mattered.

Once he found his voice, the room came alive. He had a way of illuminating the deepest, most complex ideas, turning the dense philosophy of Kant, Hegel, and especially Leibniz into something urgent and vital. He was writing a book on Leibniz, and I found myself particularly drawn to the philosopher's idea of the *pre-established harmony of the universe* – his belief in the ultimate triumph of good over evil. It was exactly the kind of hope I needed.

But Professor Huber was not just an academic. He was bold. Subversive. Even funny. Once, while lecturing on Spinoza, he said with mock caution, 'Careful, he's a Jew! Don't let yourselves be contaminated if you read him.' Nervous laughter rippled through the hall. I bit back a smile, silently cheering him on.

I last saw Fritz in the middle of May 1942. Neither of us knew it would be our final meeting. If, by some miracle, I escape my fate at the hands of the Gestapo – which I suspect I won't – and if Fritz returns safely from Russia – I pray with all my heart that he will – then there is still hope that we might see each other again. But deep down, I feel the truth in my heart: we won't meet again in this life.

Fritz was en route from France to the Eastern Front, but because he was permitted to travel independently of the company he command-ed, he adjusted his schedule and made a detour through Munich.

He couldn't stay long – just one day, he said. I sensed an unease in him, a shadow that hadn't been there before. He didn't speak much about his assignment, and I didn't press him. Perhaps he didn't want to put into words the dread that sat heavy between us. He also didn't ask whether I had put his money toward the duplicating machine. If he had, I could have answered honestly: *not yet.*

Instead, we steered clear of difficult subjects and tried to enjoy the fine weather, pretending, if only for a little while, that war wasn't pulling us in different directions.

When it was time for him to leave, his mood shifted. He became reflective, his thoughts drifting back to a time before the war had upended our lives.

'That summer on the North Sea,' he said. 'It was the best of times.'

'Three years ago,' I murmured. 'It feels more like thirty.'

We had been different people then – young, carefree, in love with the world and each other. Now, the war had left its mark on us both.

He took my hands in his. 'You'll keep writing to me, won't you, Sophie?'

'Of course,' I promised. 'And I expect you to tell me everything about Russia.'

A wry smile crossed his face. 'I will,' he said, but we both knew there were things he wouldn't be able to say.

Then, without warning, he pulled me into a fierce embrace, as if he could hold me close enough to defy time, to keep me from slipping away. 'Goodbye, Sophie, my love. Stay strong.'

He turned and walked toward the waiting train.

He didn't look back.

Fritz wrote from Mariupol. It had taken ten gruelling days to reach the southern flank of the Eastern Front. At least, he noted, he was far from the planned march on Moscow. But distance meant little in a war where the frontlines shifted like sand, and safety was an illusion.

In his letter, he described the overwhelming vastness of the landscape as he crossed the Dnieper River. The endless stretch of open land, the sky pressing down, made him feel untethered and remote from anything human. It was a landscape that filled him with both awe and a creeping terror. 'Fear oppresses my heart,' he wrote.

His arrival in Mariupol was met with a brutal welcome. As his company unloaded equipment and supplies at the station, Russian planes roared overhead, dropping bombs. By sheer luck, no one was killed or injured, but the attack was a sharp and sobering reminder: danger was everywhere, and death could strike at any moment.

As Commanding Officer, Fritz took the staff room in a local school for his quarters. His few possessions rattled around the large space: a field table, a camp stool, and a bed with mosquito netting.

He would be busy, he said, but he was determined to find time to write to me. He also promised to find an hour a day for reading, no matter what.

I clung to that promise. I hoped books would help him hold onto himself – to the man I knew, the man he truly was. I feared what war could do to a person, how easily one could be swallowed up by the relentless machinery of it all. I didn't want Fritz to become just another cog in the German war machine. I wanted him to stay Fritz.

As May melted into June, Munich shook off the last traces of spring and settled into the languid warmth of early summer. The city was alive with music – Bach's *Brandenburg Concertos*, a Beethoven symphony, the strains of Mozart drifting through concert halls. Afterward, we spilled into the beer gardens, the clink of steins and the low hum of conversation offering a brief illusion of normality. On quieter nights, we opened a bottle of wine in someone's room, talking into the early hours, seeking solace in each other's company.

The parks were ablaze with colour, the Isar shimmered in the sunlight, and people lounged on the grass, reading, chatting, soaking in the warmth. For a fleeting moment, you could almost believe the world was at peace.

But it wasn't.

The National Socialist flags hung from every public building, an unavoidable reminder of the war and the man leading us all toward destruction. British bombing campaigns were intensifying. The war was escalating. Someone needed to do something. Now.

I was growing impatient. There had been too much talk and not enough action. We had discussed, debated, analysed news reports until we were hoarse, but words weren't enough. It was time to act. But while I was ready, the others still hesitated.

Hans, for one, was preoccupied. His relationship with Traute had disintegrated after he had slept with her best friend, Ulla. He may have been my brother, but when it came to women, he could be a real cad. And yet, somehow, Traute remained in our circle, still engaging in our late-night conversations, still dissecting the war with us as we tried to make sense of it all.

Perhaps we were guilty of living in our own bubble, of believing there were many more people who thought as we did. But in those long nights, we convinced ourselves that truth was all people needed – that if they only saw the reality of the war, they would rise up against Hitler. We just had to give them the push, show them they weren't alone.

And there was also the nagging matter of my accommodation.

Lodging with Dr Muth had been a privilege – he was generous, kind, and his library was a sanctuary – but I was restless. I was cut off from the heart of Munich, removed from the action, from Hans, from my friends. I needed to be where things were happening.

Hans had offered me his room in Mandlstrasse, but he was dragging his feet about moving out. I nagged him mercilessly, and eventually, he relocated to Traute's old room in Lindwurm Strasse. I wasted no time in taking over Mandlstrasse.

Finally, I had a space of my own. A spacious room in the heart of the city, just minutes from the university on Ludwigstrasse. My landlady, Frau Lösch, even allowed me to use the telephone in the hallway – an unexpected bonus.

It felt like a shift, like the pieces were finally falling into place. The time for hesitation was over. Now, we had to act.

Frau Mertens was a well-connected woman in Munich, renowned for her *soirées*, where the city's intellectual and artistic elite gathered for lively discussions over music, literature, and fine wine. Imagine our excitement when Hans and I received an invitation to attend one of these coveted gatherings. I wasn't sure how the invitation had come about – perhaps through our association with Dr Muth – but it felt like a significant opportunity.

The guest speaker that evening was Sigismund von Radecki, the writer, satirist, and actor. Among the other distinguished guests were Professor Kurt Huber and the publisher Heinrich Ellermann. To be in such company was an honour. Traute and Christoph accompanied us, along with several other students eager for intellectual debate.

We arrived expecting an evening of refined entertainment – music, literature, perhaps a spirited discussion of philosophy over glasses of Riesling. But the night would prove far more electrifying than we had anticipated.

In the genteel setting of Frau Mertens's elegantly furnished parlour, where velvet drapes framed tall windows and a chandelier cast a warm golden glow over the guests, Radecki had us in stitches with his razor-sharp wit. His dry observations on daily life in Nazi Germany, laced with double meanings, elicited waves of laughter. For a brief time, we were transported out of the oppressive reality of the regime and into the realm of humour and subversive wordplay.

Then, just as the laughter began to subside, our hostess took to the floor.

'How does one preserve one's inner values,' she asked, her voice measured, deliberate, 'in a world of National Socialism?'

I sat up straighter, sensing Hans beside me doing the same. A hush fell over the gathering. This was no idle parlour discussion. This was something far more dangerous.

'The National Socialists speak of *innere Erneuerung*—inner renewal,' Frau Mertens continued. 'They argue that Germany needs a moral and cultural resurgence after the so-called decadence that followed our defeat in the Great War. For them, this means not only a return to so-called moral purity but also a reassertion of national strength, of pride. And of course' – she paused, letting the words settle – 'it means expanding German living space in Europe.'

Hans exhaled sharply, clenching and unclenching his fists. 'Invading other nations, more like,' he muttered, his leg bouncing with pent-up frustration.

On my other side, Christoph was frowning, deep in thought. I knew that look. He was about to speak, and I braced myself.

When Frau Mertens invited discussion, the division in the room became stark. The older guests, seasoned intellectuals, took a more cautious approach, while we students bristled with urgency.

Publisher Heinrich Ellermann was the first to respond. 'Outright resistance will achieve nothing,' he said, swirling the wine in his glass as if contemplating a purely academic problem. 'The best course is to cultivate values – morality, truth, culture – so that when this storm passes, we are ready to rebuild.' He spoke as if the Nazi era were merely an inconvenient squall, a passing rain shower over Germany's history.

Hans pounced. 'So you're saying we should rent an island in the Aegean and sit there reading world philosophy while people are arrested and executed?'

A ripple of nervous laughter passed through the younger guests. But there was no amusement in Hans's voice, only seething frustration.

I saw Professor Huber glance at Hans, his eyebrows raised in appraisal. This was the first time they had encountered each other, and I could tell Huber was intrigued.

Some guests murmured their agreement with Ellermann. What *could* be done? The Nazi machine was too powerful. The state saw everything, knew everything. Resistance was futile.

Christel could hold back no longer. His voice cut through the room. 'Are we supposed to just accept Nazi atrocities? The Allies are bombing our cities. This war cannot end well for Germany. When it's over, the world will ask – what did we *do*? What did we *do* to stop it?'

Then, to everyone's astonishment, Professor Huber, who had sat quietly until now, suddenly erupted: 'Something must be done. And the sooner, the better!'

A stunned silence fell over the room.

Hans turned toward him, their eyes locking in unspoken understanding.

'Yes,' Hans said, his voice steady, his conviction unwavering. 'We have to act.'

And in that moment, the course of our lives shifted irreversibly.

Despite his promise to find time to write, nearly two weeks passed before Fritz was finally able to put pen to paper. His absence had stretched unbearably long, but when his letter arrived, I devoured every word. He had been away from the base in Mariupol, deep in the Ukrainian countryside, installing communication equipment near the front lines.

He described a harrowing journey. He had flown to Kharkiv in a *Storch* plane, a small, lightweight aircraft known for its ability to take off and land in the tightest of spaces. But even a *Storch* needed fuel. Mid-flight, they ran out. The pilot had no choice but to make an emergency landing, the plane lurching down into unfamiliar terrain.

That was only the beginning of their ordeal. Back in the air after re-fuelling, the navigator lost his bearings, and they ended up 120 miles off course, wandering over the vast, open steppe with no clear direction. When they finally corrected their route, the weather turned against them. A storm rolled in and, in Fritz's words, 'It made our little bird dance.' I could picture him gripping his seat as the plane bucked and swayed, tossed like a leaf in the wind.

Yet even through the turbulence – both literal and figurative – Fritz's eye for beauty remained. He wrote with wonder about the landscape sprawling beneath him, how he wished he could have taken pictures of the Dnieper River from the sky. He was captivated by the sight of Ukrainian villages – whitewashed houses with thatched roofs nestled in the rolling countryside. And the churches, their onion-domed towers twisting skyward.

There was an unexpected lightness in his letter too – an anecdote that made me laugh out loud. A Russian variety performance had been arranged for the German soldiers, and Fritz had looked forward to hearing folksongs, witnessing traditional dances, and perhaps catching a glimpse of authentic Russian culture. Instead, what he got was a bawdy cabaret act, the kind of lowbrow entertainment he might have stumbled across in a seedy backstreet club in Berlin. He wrote:

I feel like I belong somewhere else.

I paused when I read that line. The words were simple, but they carried so much weight. He was far from home, stranded in a war he had never truly believed in.

I pitied him. But at the same time, I was relieved. His unease meant he was still thinking, still questioning. He had not allowed himself to be swallowed whole by the war. Not yet.

It was an evening in late June when four of us – Hans, Alex, Christoph, and I – gathered in Hans's room. As the long summer twilight stretched into night, the men smoked their pipes, I made the tea, and together we talked ourselves into revolution.

The evening at Frau Mertens's had set something alight in us. We could no longer allow our discussions to remain just that – discussions. Even Professor Huber had said that *something had to be done.* There was no time to lose.

Hans was restless, pacing the small room, unable to sit still for long. 'We have to expose what's happening,' he said, his voice urgent. 'If people knew about the war crimes, if they understood the truth, there *would* be a revolution.'

I believed him. Trusted him completely. There was no hesitation in my heart – doing nothing would be the real crime.

Alex, usually so composed, sucked on his pipe and ran a hand through his dark hair. He leaned forward, his elbows on his knees. 'Think of the risks,' he said. His voice, normally filled with dry wit, carried an uncharacteristic note of uncertainty. 'The truth will come out sooner or later. Hitler can't keep his crimes hidden forever.'

'How long will that take?' said Hans impatiently. 'Every day, people are dying. Look at what's happening in Russia.'

Alex flinched. Hans had touched a nerve. Russia was his birthplace, the land of his childhood. His silence was answer enough.

'Anything we can do to shorten the war,' I said, 'has to be worth trying.'

Christoph exhaled slowly. 'We just need to be *careful*. If the Gestapo catch wind of this, we're dead.'

'We'll keep it between the four of us,' Hans assured him. 'No one else.'

'What about Traute?' I asked. If there was anyone we could trust, it was her.

'Not yet,' Hans said. He turned to Alex. 'Are you in?'

Alex hesitated only a second. Then he nodded. 'You know you can count on me.'

Relief flooded through me. *We were doing this.* Finally, after so much talk, we would take action. I poured another round of tea, and we launched into a strategy session.

What to write? Who to target? How to print and distribute enough copies to make a real impact?

This wasn't some school essay. Our words had to *change* minds. They had to cut through years of Nazi propaganda and pierce the apathy that had settled like a disease over the country. They needed to land in the hands of people who would *act* – not just read, but *pass them on,* spread them, share them.

We decided that Hans and Alex would each draft a leaflet, then we would refine them together.

In the end, the first leaflet was unmistakably Hans's work. His mind brimmed with philosophy, literature, and the weight of history. From the opening line, he was uncompromising:

> *Nothing is more unworthy of a civilized nation than to let itself be governed without resistance by an irresponsible clique ruled by dark instincts. Is it not true that every honest German is ashamed of their government today? And what shame will fall upon us and our children when the veil is lifted and the unspeakable crimes – crimes beyond human comprehension – are revealed to the world?*

He laid bare the moral corruption of a nation that allowed itself to be enslaved. He did not hold back, sounding at times like an Old Testament prophet foretelling doom:

> *If everyone waits till someone else makes a start, the messengers of the avenging Nemesis will draw incessantly closer. And then the last sacrifice will have been thrown senselessly into the jaws of the insatiable demon. Therefore in this last hour every individual must arm himself as best he can, aware of his responsibility as a member of the Christian and western civilization. He must work against the scourge of humanity, against fascism and all similar systems of an absolute State.*

We advocated passive resistance to hinder the war machine, before it was too late. Before our cities lay in ruins like Cologne and before the last of our young people had bled to death. Hans warned:

> *Do not forget that every nation deserves the government*
> *that it endures.*

Then he quoted from the greats of German literature. He borrowed from Schiller, whose words rang with truth:

> *'The state is never an end in itself. It is important only*
> *as a means by which humanity can achieve its goal,*
> *which is nothing other than the advancement of man's*
> *constructive capabilities.'*

And from Goethe's *The Awakening of Epimenides:*

> *That which has arisen bravely from the pit*
> *Can conquer half the globe*
> *With a pitiless destiny,*
> *But return it must to the abyss.*
> *...*
> *The lovely word of freedom*
> *Is spoken lisping and stammering*
> *Until in unaccustomed newness*
> *We stand upon our temple steps*
> *And cry anew enraptured:*
> *Freedom!*

> *Freedom!*
> *Freedom!*

As a final instruction, Hans wrote:

> *We ask that you copy this document, making as many*
> *carbon copies as possible, and pass it on!*

When Hans finished reading, no one spoke for a long moment. The air felt charged.

Then Christoph exhaled and rubbed his forehead. 'You *do* realise we're risking our necks, don't you?'

Hans nodded. 'We've known that all along.'

Alex tapped the ashes from his pipe and smiled wryly. 'Well, if we're going to die, let's make it count.'

And so it began.

Writing the words was only the first step. Now came the real challenge: distribution.

Who should receive a copy? It had to go to people who would listen, people with the power to influence others, people who would pass it on in turn. We selected academics – among them, Professor Huber – who we believed would be sympathetic to our cause. To reach beyond our immediate circle, we also picked random addresses from the phone book.

Alex, ever resourceful, borrowed a typewriter – an American Remington – from his neighbour, a committed Nazi. 'For academic work,' he told the man, feigning nonchalance. He had learned to lie with a straight face. Some of the leaflets would inevitably fall into the hands of the Gestapo, and the last thing he wanted was for them to be traced back to his family's typewriter.

The final leaflet was four pages long. We planned to distribute at least a hundred copies. Carbon paper wouldn't suffice. We needed something more efficient.

Pooling our money and the money from Fritz, we bought a basic duplicating machine. Alex also secured four hundred sheets of paper, wax stencils, envelopes, and postage stamps. The logistics were falling into place, but something was missing.

'We need a way to identify ourselves,' Alex mused one evening, leaning back in his chair, pipe in hand. Smoke curled around his face, drifting toward the ceiling. 'Something that sets us apart but keeps our real names hidden.'

I watched him as he spoke, mesmerised by his quiet intensity. There was something magnetic about him – something utterly *different* from anyone else I knew. His sharp features, the high forehead and unruly hair, the languid elegance of his movements. He belonged nowhere and everywhere.

He was the antithesis of the rigid German ideal. He hated the uniformity of the Third Reich, its blind conformity, its soulless obedience. His refusal to fit in was apparent in everything – the way his hair flopped boyishly to the side, defying the cropped styles of the Hitler Youth; the way he dressed in riding breeches and turtleneck sweaters rather than the stiff military garb forced upon him. Even his voice, deep and melodious, carried a Russian inflection, an echo of his childhood in the Urals. Russian blood ran through him, shaping his very essence. He sang Russian folksongs accompanying himself on the balalaika, devoured Dostoevsky, and felt more at home among vagabonds and gypsies than among his own people.

And I loved him for it.

Not that it mattered. I belonged to Fritz, who was risking his life on the Eastern Front. And Alex – Alex was in love with Lilo Ramdohr, the artist who was married to someone else. A hopeless tangle. We were all so much better at fighting for justice than navigating our own emotions.

Alex exhaled another plume of smoke, then suddenly sat up. 'I've got it,' he declared, startling me out of my thoughts. He sprang to his feet and began rifling through stacks of notepaper.

Hans smirked. 'Well, don't keep us in suspense.'

Alex stuck his pipe back into his mouth, one hand still rummaging. 'I wrote it down somewhere... Ah! Here it is.' He plucked a page from the chaos and held it aloft.

Christoph raised an eyebrow. 'What is that?'

Alex glanced down at the paper, then back at us, a glint of satisfaction in his eyes. 'It's from a letter Fritz Rook sent to Lilo.'

'She lets you read her private letters?' Christoph sounded both amused and appalled.

Alex merely shrugged. 'Lilo shares everything she finds beautiful. Listen.'

He cleared his throat and read aloud:

> *Yesterday, late in the evening, I spied a white rose. It is said that white flowers are for the dead – but death, love, and youth are all one and the same. Therefore it is precisely the white rose with its fragrance and its fragile purity that is the symbol of eternal youth.*

'Beautiful,' I breathed. I wished someone would write lines like that to me. 'The White Rose. Shall we call ourselves that?'

'Yes,' said Hans firmly. 'It fits.'

And just like that, we had our name.

We typed *Leaflets of the White Rose I* at the top of the first leaflet. We were in business.

Chapter Nineteen

February 1943

A guard fetches me from the cell. I assume it's for another round of questioning, but instead, he takes me to a different room. The air is heavy with stale cigarette smoke, the walls bare and pitiless.

An official stands before me, his expression blank as he hands me a stack of typed pages.

'This is your indictment. Read it.'

I sit, my hands trembling as I take the document. My breath comes shallow as I begin to read.

Three names. Hans Scholl. Sophie Scholl. Christoph Probst.

The indictment begins with an almost polite acknowledgment that none of us has any prior convictions. As if that will count for anything now. As if that will save us. Then comes the list of charges, laid out in cold, bureaucratic precision.

Firstly, high treason – for attempting to overthrow the Reich by force.

By force? The absurdity of it almost makes me laugh. We, a handful of students armed with nothing but words, are accused of trying to bring down an empire built on tanks, bombs, and blood.

Secondly, aiding the enemies of the Reich – for allegedly weakening Germany's war effort.

If only we *had* possessed the power to aid the Allies. If only we had been able to strike a blow strong enough to end the war, to stop the killing, to bring everything crashing down before it was too late.

Thirdly, undermining the morale of the German people – for attempting to turn them against their government.

That much, at least, is true. We wanted to wake them up, shake them from their stupor, make them see what was happening in their name. We wanted them to resist.

The indictment describes Hans's role in writing and distributing the leaflets, my own involvement in the same, and Christoph's single act – his draft of a leaflet. That is all it takes to condemn us.

Then, under the section titled *Significant Conclusion of the Investigations*, I see my father's name, citing his former role as the mayor of Forchtenberg and his work as a business consultant in Ulm. They list our siblings – Inge, Elisabeth, Werner. They haven't forgotten the previous arrests. They note Hans's personal journey: from school, to the Hitler Youth, to the army, to medical school.

And me? I am a former kindergarten teacher and student. My role as a Group Leader in the League of German Girls is given a single, brief mention, as if to mock how far I have strayed from the path expected of me.

Finally, there is Christoph. A medical student. A soldier. But not a husband, not a father of three small children. There is no mention of his wife, still recovering from childbirth, nor of the newborn who may never know his father.

The indictment cites from the leaflets directly, the words bringing back so many memories. The 'alleged' murder of Jews; the 'alleged' deportation of Poles; our calls for passive resistance; our calls for sabotage; our belief that the war was nearing its end, that an invasion from the West was imminent, that Hitler could not possibly win the war, only prolong it. All this I still believe to be true.

Alexander Schmorell is named as a co-conspirator, working alongside Hans. My dearest wish is that Alex has escaped from Germany. He is brave and resourceful. If he can make it across the Alps to Switzerland, he will be safe. I send up a prayer to God for Alex's deliverance.

My eyes start to glaze over as I read about Hans's political views and my own role in purchasing stationery. It's all rather tedious and pedantic. What the report contains in facts, it utterly lacks in emotion. Then I read:

> *She accompanied her brother to the university, was observed scattering the leaflets, and was apprehended along with him.*

My stomach clenches. What moment of madness caused me to scatter the leaflets from the balustrade? If I hadn't done that, Schmidt wouldn't have noticed us. The lectures would have finished and we would have merged with the other students and made our way out of the building. We would have been free to continue our work. If only...

But *if only* changes nothing.

I've read enough. I push the indictment away, my hands cold and stiff. The official watches me impassively before nodding to the guard.

Back in the cell, Else is waiting for me. I wander over to the window and gaze outside. The sky is clear blue.

'It's such a lovely, sunny day,' I say. 'And yet, I have to go.'

'Please, don't say that.' Her voice wavers. She comes to stand beside me, her presence warm and steady.

'It's true,' I murmur. 'How many are dying today on the battle-fields? How many young men, full of hope, are being torn to pieces by this war? What does my death matter, if it stirs even a few into action?'

Else swallows hard. There are tears in her eyes. 'Oh, Sophie, don't give up hope. You might get a long sentence. Maybe they will take your youth into account. Maybe – '

She stops herself. We both know the truth.

I shake my head. 'If Hans is sentenced to death, then my sentence should be no different. I am as guilty as he is.'

Else grips my hand, holding on as if she can keep me tethered to this world. But we both know that I am already slipping away.

Chapter Twenty

June – July 1942

The first leaflet was printed – one hundred copies – carefully folded, sealed in envelopes, and posted.

What did we expect? That the recipients would be so stirred by our words that they would rush to make copies, passing them on to friends and family, who in turn would do the same? That soon, a wave of resistance would sweep across Germany, growing stronger with each passing day?

Perhaps it was naive, but in our hearts, that was exactly what we hoped for.

Despite their growing estrangement, Hans couldn't resist showing a copy to Traute after a lecture. He didn't tell her he had written it – only handed it to her with a casual, 'Read this and tell me what you think.'

She scanned the page, her brow furrowing as she read. When she finished, she looked up, her eyes gleaming with admiration.

'Someone very intelligent wrote this,' she said. I can imagine the pride that must have flickered across Hans's face.

But Traute knew him too well. She studied him for a moment, then asked directly, 'It was you, wasn't it?'

Hans's easy smile didn't waver. 'You shouldn't ask who wrote it,' he said lightly. 'It's too dangerous to know.'

Traute held his gaze. 'It *was* you,' she murmured, as if the words were a certainty rather than a question.

Her approval was gratifying, but there was someone whose reaction mattered more. We wanted to impress Professor Huber.

Hans and Alex decided to invite him to one of the literary soirées at Alex's house.

The Schmorell villa in Benediktenwand Strasse was in the south of Munich, in the leafy suburb of Harlaching. It was a house where conversations stretched long into the night, where books lined the walls and a grand piano stood in the salon. For those of us who despised the regime, it felt like a rare refuge. I loved going there. The garden, surrounded by a high wall, was in full bloom, the scent of summer roses filling the warm air.

That evening, as guests mingled on the veranda, I met Willi Graf for the first time. Christoph and Alex introduced him as a fellow medical student, quiet and serious, his solemnity at odds with Alex's usual rakish charm. He seemed hesitant at first, but I sensed a deep conviction beneath his reserved manner. He, too, hated the Nazis. But we never spoke about the White Rose to anyone beyond our circle.

Eventually, Hans and Traute arrived with Professor Huber. He shuffled up the garden path, glancing around as though he had not expected to find himself in such a grand setting. He looked older than I remembered from his lectures – pale, a little worn, his right leg dragging slightly. He was not a man who sought out society. I knew from Hans that he lived modestly in Gräfelfing with his wife and children. His refusal to join the Nazi Party had cost him professional advancement. That, more than anything, made us believe he might be sympathetic to our cause.

Hans introduced him to the group, and he shook hands politely, though he seemed uneasy. We took our seats inside the salon, sinking into the deep chairs, the air thick with the scent of pipe smoke and fresh coffee. I watched him, waiting, trying to gauge his thoughts.

At first, we spoke of books, art, philosophy. The usual topics. But we had invited him for something more.

It was Traute who finally broached the subject. 'Have you seen one of those White Rose leaflets?' she asked, her tone casual. 'They've been appearing all over the place.'

Professor Huber flinched. His head trembled slightly. 'Yes,' he said after a long pause. 'I received one.'

Hans leaned forward. 'And?'

Huber hesitated, then said, 'I don't think something like that is going to have much impact. It's almost certainly not worth the risk.'

His words hit like a slap.

Hans, ever the master of control, smiled as though the response did not wound him. Alex blew a slow ring of smoke into the air. Christoph frowned, deep in thought.

We moved on to other topics – university policies, the war, the slow suffocation of intellectual life. Hans tried, more than once, to draw Huber into something deeper, but he remained guarded, limiting his remarks to academic concerns. He bemoaned the decline of true scientific research, lamented the lack of intellectual freedom. But when the conversation steered too close to the realm of direct action, he fell silent.

Finally, he stood, thanked the Schmorells for an 'interesting evening,' and excused himself. His wife was expecting him home.

The room felt emptier after he left.

Later, when most of the guests had gone, we gathered to talk.

'He was hopeless,' Alex muttered, shaking his head.

'I must say, I was rather disappointed,' Christoph admitted. 'I thought he'd be keener to speak his mind.'

Hans, thoughtful as ever, ran a hand through his hair. 'I don't know,' he said slowly. 'Maybe he just needs more time. We won't give up on him.' I saw the determination in his eyes, the quiet resolve that had carried us this far. 'Yes,' he murmured. 'I think he'll come around.'

We got to know the architect Manfred Eickemeyer through a mutual friend of Carl Muth's. Manfred spent most of his time working in Kraków, now the capital of the General Government in Poland under Hitler's lawyer, Hans Frank. He was one of the few people we trusted enough to let in on our secret work. In his absence, he let us use his studio on Leopoldstrasse to type and print our leaflets.

On one of his rare visits back to Munich, he sat with us in Hans's apartment, his face grave.

'The SS are killing the Jews,' he said.

Silence fell. We had expected something terrible, but not this.

Hans leaned forward. 'What do you mean?'

'They round them up, drive them outside the cities, force them to dig trenches, and then shoot them. The bodies fall into the trenches.'

Hans clenched his fists. 'And the Wehrmacht?'

'They do nothing,' Manfred said bitterly. 'They look the other way.'

Hans and Alex exchanged glances. Manfred leaned forward, looking each of us in the eye. 'You have to write about this. People need to know.'

'We will,' Hans said firmly.

That evening, we set to work, the room filling with the scent of pipe smoke. Hans paced the floor, too restless to sit. Alex lounged in an armchair, one leg draped over the side, pipe dangling from his lips. I made tea, listening, absorbing every word.

'It's impossible to have an intellectual debate about National Socialism,' Hans said, running a hand through his hair. 'There's no rational basis for it.'

'Exactly,' Alex agreed. 'It's built on deception and betrayal. The whole system is corrupt. The Nazis lie to us constantly.'

Hans pulled a tattered copy of *Mein Kampf* from the bookshelf and flipped through the pages. 'Here it is,' he said, tapping a passage. '"It is unbelievable to what extent one must betray a people in order to rule it."' He snapped the book shut. 'Hitler wrote that, openly. And people still followed him.'

Alex exhaled a plume of smoke. 'Were they blind? Deaf? Did they not *want* to see?'

'National Socialism is like a disease,' Hans muttered, grabbing a scrap of paper and scribbling down the thought. 'Like a cancer that has infected the entire nation.'

I watched them closely, their minds sparking off each other. Hans, feverish with purpose, pacing like a caged animal. Alex, languid in posture but sharp with intensity.

'What about Poland?' I said. 'Manfred told us what's happening to the Jews there. We *have* to write about that.'

Hans nodded, flipping the paper over. 'Three hundred thousand Jews already murdered.'

'Just a number,' Alex said. 'People will pity them, but they need to feel *guilt*.'

'Yes.' Hans scribbled another note. 'Guilt. Shame. Responsibility.'

'But we also need hope,' I said. 'If we only condemn, they'll turn away. We have to tell them it's not too late to act.'

Hans wrote furiously. 'It is the duty of every German citizen to *destroy* these beasts.'

'That works,' I agreed.

By the time the drafts were done, both Hans and Alex had written versions in their own styles, weaving together philosophy, history, and moral outrage. They read through each other's work and combined the best parts into a final draft. This time, they ended with two quotations from Lao-Tzu – on the nature of good and bad government – and a plea to make as many copies as possible and pass them on.

Hans typed up the final version. I prepared the stencils and began the laborious task of cranking out the copies, one by one, on the mimeograph machine. How many hours did I spend at that handle, pressing down, lifting, pressing down again? The ink smudged my fingers, my wrist ached, and the muscles in my arm grew stiff. But I didn't stop.

On the last day of June, we sent out the leaflets, selecting names at random from the phone book.

A few days later, Manfred read a copy. He looked up, his expression unreadable.

'You should have included more details about the deaths in Poland,' he said. 'This is too vague.'

Hans frowned. 'Three hundred thousand murdered isn't enough?'

Manfred shook his head. 'People won't believe it. It's just a number to them. They'll dismiss it as exaggeration, enemy propaganda. You need names, places, something *concrete*. Otherwise, people will think you're scaremongering.'

We listened in silence. He was right. We still had a lot to learn.

Fritz continued to write to me from Russia, even though my letters to him were no longer getting through.

> *I don't know how you are or if you are enjoying Munich.*
> *I keep hoping for word from you.*

He appreciated being stationed in a quieter part of the country, far from the worst of the fighting. But at the same time, the monotony was wearing him down. He loathed the empty conversations with drunken officers, their crude jokes, their casual cruelty. He was surrounded by men who had numbed themselves to the horrors around them. Fritz was different – he could still feel, still question, still pray.

Then, finally, a batch of my letters reached him. Four at once.

> *I read them all in one sitting. Every word. Over and*
> *over. Nothing can separate us, Sophie.*

But it was another of his letters that convinced me – *as if I needed convincing!* – that writing our leaflets was the right thing to do.

His commanding officer had spoken about the slaughter of Jews in occupied Russia with cold, bureaucratic detachment, as if he were discussing the weather or supply shortages. He described the mass executions without flinching, without hesitation, as if the systematic murder of entire families was simply another logistical task to be completed.

Fritz was horrified.

How can anyone think this is right? How does a man
become so empty, so blind?

He could not speak out. But he could still write to me. He could
still pray to God.

And I knew, more than ever, that I had to act.

I remember how utterly exhausting those days of June and July were,
in the relentless heat of Munich. When we weren't studying, we were
working on White Rose tasks, stealing moments between lectures to
prepare our next leaflet. The days blurred together, an endless cycle of
writing, printing, and distributing.

My job was to buy paper, stamps, and envelopes. To avoid suspicion, I never bought too much from one place. Instead, I visited
different shops, pretending to be just another student preparing for
her studies. But I was never at ease. Every time I stepped into a shop,
my pulse quickened. Was someone watching? Would the shopkeeper
remember my face? Would the Gestapo come knocking at my door?
As soon as I returned home, I hid my purchases in a drawer, out of
sight but never out of mind.

Hans and Alex worked tirelessly on drafting and refining the third
leaflet. After Herr Eickemeyer's critique of the last one, Hans was
determined to make this one sharper, more compelling. He wanted to
hammer home the idea that a just state must reflect divine order – that
every human being deserved a government that protected both individual freedom and the common good. It was God's will that people

should live free and independent lives while also standing together in solidarity. Instead, we were living under a *'dictatorship of evil.'*

Passive resistance, we argued, was the key to defeating National Socialism. There was no point in fighting Bolshevism when the real enemy was within our own borders. Germany *must not* be allowed to win the war.

Of course, we couldn't tell people exactly what to do, but we could show them how small acts of defiance could help bring down the Nazi regime. We called for sabotage in every corner of society—disrupting Nazi assemblies, rallies, and ceremonies; obstructing scientific research that fuelled the war effort; undermining cultural institutions and the arts that promoted fascist ideology. We urged people to refuse to donate to public fund-raising drives.

> *Do not give your metal. Do not give your textiles. Every contribution prolongs the war.*

This time, we quoted Aristotle:

> *'Tyrants employ spies everywhere because they must know what their subjects are saying and doing at all times. They create division in society by setting people against each other.'*

Surely, the parallel to Hitler's Germany was obvious.

We knew some people would hand their leaflets straight to the Gestapo. We expected it. But we also believed – *we had to believe* – that others would have the courage to pass them on.

Once every word was scrutinised and refined, we prepared the stencils. Traute joined me in printing, taking turns cranking the mimeograph machine until our arms ached. Then came the long hours of stuffing leaflets into envelopes, pressing stamps onto corners.

And then, at last, we slipped out into the night, moving through the city with quiet purpose, depositing our leaflets in post boxes across Munich. Each envelope was a small act of defiance.

We didn't know if people would listen. We didn't know if it would make a difference. But we did it anyway.

The summer semester was slipping through our fingers in a whirlwind of lectures, essays, concerts, and White Rose activities. Hans and Alex were determined to write a fourth leaflet before the holidays, but just as our momentum was building, we received frustrating news: Hans, Alex, Willi, and several of our friends would be going to Russia as part of a medical corps.

Alex, ever the romantic, was elated at the thought of finally showing his friends his beloved Russia. But the rest of us felt the sting of having to put our work on hold before we'd truly achieved anything.

There was no time to lose on the fourth leaflet.

'We can't ignore the fact,' said Alex, 'that the newspapers are filled with talk of German victories. Africa, Russia – the Reich is celebrating its conquests.'

'Then we acknowledge it,' said Hans. 'But we remind people of the price. Who is counting the dead?'

Alex exhaled sharply, his fingers tightening around his pipe. 'Thousands are dying every day in Russia. It's like a reaper cutting through a harvest with wide strokes. There is mourning in country cottages. Mothers are crying, and there is no one to dry their tears.'

Hans's eyes lit up. 'That's brilliant. Write that down.'

The deeper Hans delved into his Christian faith, the more convinced he was we were not merely fighting against a political regime – we were battling against something darker, something insidious.

'Hitler is Satan walking the earth,' he said. 'National Socialism is the work of the Antichrist. Demons lurk in the shadows, preying on mankind's weakness. But God has given us the strength to resist. It is our duty to fight.'

His fervour sent shivers down my spine.

'We should make one thing clear,' Hans continued. 'We're not being funded by any foreign power. We know the Nazis can only be defeated militarily. But that's not our fight. Our fight is to renew the German spirit. But first' – he slammed his palm against the table – 'people must recognise their own guilt. They must wake up to what they've allowed to happen.' His voice softened slightly. 'There is no earthly punishment great enough for Hitler and his followers. But they *must* be punished. They *must* be held accountable – not just for justice, but to make sure no one ever follows this path again.'

That night, Hans worked tirelessly, his fingers flying across the typewriter keys, hammering out the final draft.

We ended with a warning:

> *We will not be silent. We are your bad conscience. The White Rose will not leave you in peace!*

Traute and I prepared the stencils, cranking out as many copies as we could, our hands cramping from the effort. We stuffed the leaflets into envelopes and posted them across the city.

And then, it was time to stop.

We cleared out the cellar in Manfred Eickemeyer's studio, wiping away every trace of our existence. By the time we were done, it was as if the White Rose had never been there at all.

But the words we had written – those could never be erased.

The evening before Hans, Alex, and Willi were due to leave for Russia, we gathered in Manfred's studio for a farewell party. It felt strangely subdued, as if we were all aware that something was shifting, that nothing would be quite the same when they returned – *if* they returned.

Professor Huber joined us, looking far more at ease in the relaxed atmosphere of the studio than he had at the Schmorells' grand villa. We sprawled on pillows and chairs, a bottle of schnapps making the rounds, while Alex poured wine with his usual flair. Someone had brought a cake. We spoke of art and literature, but politics was always there, lurking beneath the surface, like a shadow that couldn't be ignored.

Alex, pipe clenched between his teeth, exhaled a swirl of blue smoke into the air. 'The only way to survive right now,' he mused, 'is through passive resistance.'

'I agree,' said Professor Huber, gripping his glass as his hands trembled. 'If we were workers, we could strike. But what can intellectuals do? If we refuse to teach or write, no one will miss us. The best we can do is boycott Nazi functions, keep our heads down, and wait for this madness to burn itself out.'

Hans shook his head, his jaw tightening. 'That's not enough. We don't have the luxury of waiting. We need to prepare for the overthrow of this regime *now*.'

The weight of those words pressed down on all of us. We knew how dangerous it was even to *think* such things, let alone speak them aloud.

Professor Huber took a deep, unsteady breath. 'And what will be left?' he asked. 'The destruction of German cities is already dreadful.' He was referring, of course, to the relentless Allied bombings. 'What's going to be left of our great cultural traditions?'

'Oh, to hell with *cultural traditions*,' Manfred snapped, shaking his head in disgust. He was on leave from Kraków and had seen too much. 'The German people *deserve* what's happening to them.'

A stunned silence fell over the room.

Manfred set down his glass with a thud and looked around at us. 'You don't understand. You *cannot* understand. I've *seen* it. The mass executions. The SS getting drunk after murdering entire villages. Jews packed into the Warsaw Ghetto like animals. The streets are filled with death. And what are the Wehrmacht doing?' He gave a hollow laugh. 'Nothing. They stand by and let it happen.'

Professor Huber's hands shook so violently that wine sloshed over the edge of his glass. His voice, when it came, was almost a whisper. 'We need... clandestine propaganda. Effective sabotage. And' – he hesitated – 'assassination!'

Stunned silence.

I wondered then if Hans was going to tell Professor Huber about the White Rose, but he said nothing.

The spell was broken by a knock at the door. Hans Hirzel, my friend Susanne's brother from Ulm, had come to say goodbye. A few more drinks were poured, but the mood had shifted.

I didn't want Hans, Alex, and Willi to go to Russia. I was terrified of what awaited them there. Fritz was already fighting on the Eastern Front, and although his letters never told the full truth, I could read between the lines. But Alex, with his Russian soul, was feverish with anticipation. He spoke of the trip as if it were a pilgrimage, a chance to reach out in friendship rather than war.

Willi, ever quiet, said nothing.

The party broke up early.

At the door, Professor Huber shook hands with Hans, Alex, and Willi. 'You *will* write to me,' he insisted, 'about your impressions from the battlefields?'

Hans promised that he would.

I barely slept that night.

At dawn, I cycled to the *Ostbahnhof* to see them off.

Goodbyes are always impossible. You stand around, heart brimming with too much emotion, words hovering on your tongue but never spoken. Time stretches unbearably slow, and then – suddenly – it's over. The moment of departure is upon you, and you find you've said nothing that truly matters.

For those leaving, there is only the pull of the journey ahead. For those staying behind, there is only the ache of watching them go.

I had no words to explain how much these people meant to me. Even Hans – whom I had known all my life – had become more than just my brother. The work we had done together, the risks we had taken, had bound us tighter than anything before.

I would have gone with them if I could.

An order was shouted. It was time to board.

Hans slung his massive rucksack over his shoulders. I hugged him fiercely and made him promise to take care of himself. He laughed, but his eyes were serious.

Then they were walking away, their backs disappearing down the platform.

I stood motionless, watching until the whistle blew and the train pulled out in a cloud of steam.

I cycled back through the quiet streets, back to my room, where I packed my suitcase in silence.

Hans was heading for his next adventure.

And for now, there was nothing left for me to do but return home to Ulm.

Chapter Twenty-One

February 1943

That evening, the cell door creaks open, and I have a visitor.

'Good evening, Sophie.' The man looks nervous, shifting from foot to foot, and jumps when the guard locks the door behind him. 'I'm, um... your defence lawyer,' he says, as if he's not entirely convinced of the fact himself.

The man standing before me is young – too young, I think, to be defending someone in a case like mine.

It's on the tip of my tongue to ask if he's even qualified yet, but I hold back. No sense in making him even more flustered than he already is. Still, I can't help but wonder – if this is the man tasked with defending me against the full force of the National Socialist state, then what hope do I have?

'Nice to meet you,' I say politely. We sit at the small, rickety table.

He clears his throat and launches into what I assume is his prepared strategy. 'I've studied the indictment,' he says, pulling out a few sheets of paper. 'If we can prove that you did not personally participate in the production of these leaflets, then I really think–'

'Wait.' I hold up a hand to stop him. 'But I *did* participate. I helped to copy and distribute them.'

He blinks at me, clearly thrown. 'Yes, well… I mean…' He frowns in confusion. 'If you're going to admit to that, then there's really nothing I can do for you.'

'So you can only help me if I lie?'

'No! That's not what I meant, I mean…' He falters, struggling to regain his footing.

I wait.

Finally, he exhales and asks, 'Why are you so ready to admit your guilt?'

'Because it's the truth.'

He stares at me as if I've just spoken a language he doesn't understand.

After a moment, I lean forward. 'But I do have a question for you.'

He nods quickly, eager for something concrete to latch onto. 'Yes, of course. What is it?'

'My brother Hans is a soldier in the Wehrmacht,' I say. 'If found guilty, will he be entitled to death by firing squad?'

He blanches. 'I – well – I don't… I mean, possibly, but that would depend…'

'And what about me?' I press.

He looks even more alarmed. 'What about you?'

'If I'm found guilty, will I be hanged in public? Or will they send me to the guillotine?'

I see the way his hands grip the edge of the table, how the colour rushes to his face. He wasn't expecting this. He wasn't expecting me.

'I... I really couldn't say,' he stammers. 'It's not my place to know these things. I...' His voice trails off.

For a moment, we just look at each other.

I offer him the smallest of smiles. 'I appreciate your honesty.'

He glances toward the door as if he can't wait to escape. 'I'll see you in court tomorrow.' He stands abruptly, knocking the table with his knee in his haste.

And just like that, he's gone.

I sit in silence for a moment, staring at the empty space where he sat. So *that's* my defence. A bumbling lawyer who would rather I lie and who can't answer a simple question.

When Else returns, I'm relieved to have her company. I wish we had more time together – to talk, to truly know each other.

Tomorrow, I will stand before a court whose authority I do not recognise.

The light burns all night, but I fall asleep almost as soon as my head hits the pillow.

Chapter Twenty-Two

August – September 1942

The moment I stepped off the train, I felt the weight of home settle over me – familiar yet confining, like a coat I had outgrown. After so much freedom in Munich, it was hard to be back under my parents' roof, walking the same streets I had known since childhood, slipping back into the quiet routines of family life. Home was comforting in some ways, but I missed my friends. Most of all, I missed the *White Rose* and our work. We had only just begun, and now everything was on hold.

I couldn't share any of this with Inge, Liesl, or my parents. The fewer people who knew, the safer they would be.

There were other worries, too.

Mother's health had taken a turn for the worse – her heart, always delicate, seemed to bear the weight of every new anxiety. If she had known what Hans and I were doing in Munich, it might have been too much for her. As it was, Father's impending trial was causing her enough distress. The charge: making disparaging remarks about Hitler and the war. The trial was set for the third of August. It loomed over us all like a gathering storm.

Inge was especially distraught. I suggested she go to Munich and ask Carl Muth to pray for Father. She took my advice, and when she returned, she was noticeably calmer.

Father, for his part, approached the whole thing with a characteristic practicality. He expected to go to prison, so he made arrangements. His friend Eugen Grimminger, an accountant in Stuttgart, would take over his practice in his absence. Grimminger was a man we trusted, a Lutheran who had married a Jewish woman, Jenny Stern. He despised Hitler as much as we did.

The morning of the trial, Father dressed in his usual suit and tie, ate his breakfast, and prepared to meet his fate with dignity. He turned to me as he adjusted his cufflinks, his deep brown eyes steady but tinged with sadness.

'Look after your mother, Sophie.'

I swallowed hard. 'I will.' I wanted to say more, but the words wouldn't come.

The verdict was as expected. He was found guilty of perfidy and sentenced to four months in prison. It could have been worse. We had to hope that after four months, he wouldn't simply be transferred to a concentration camp.

Father was strong. Mother was not. When she heard the sentence, she fell into a state of near-collapse. Inge and I helped her into bed, coaxing her back to life with warm soups and cups of tea, but she barely responded.

I wanted to stay by her side, but there was something I had to do first.

The next day, I caught the train back to Munich. Hans's room and mine needed to be cleared out – immediately. If the Gestapo came looking, they must find nothing.

With Traute's help, I worked quickly. We stripped the desks, emptied the shelves, gathered every scrap of paper, every book, every note that could be considered incriminating. Envelopes, stamps – anything that might tie us to the *White Rose*. The spare leaflets we hadn't yet distributed, we burned.

Only when the flames had consumed the last of the evidence did I return to Ulm, where Inge and I continued nursing Mother.

Father's imprisonment came with strict conditions. He was permitted to receive one letter every two weeks and could write to us only once a month. I filled my letters with encouragement and defiance, reminding him of the words he had instilled in us:

Allen Gewalten zum Trotz, sich erhalten.

Stand tall against all forces, and survive.

In the evenings, when the air cooled and the city settled into silence, I took my flute to the edge of the prison. I stood outside and played *Die Gedanken sind frei* – Thoughts Are Free – a song from the 1848 revolution. The high, clear notes carried through the night, over the walls, into the darkness.

I could only hope that the sound reached him. That, even for a moment, it reminded him that he was not alone.

To qualify for my studies in the autumn, I was required to spend August and September working in a munitions factory. The assignment filled me with dread. The only consolation was that the factory was in

Ulm, near the train station, which meant I could at least live at home and keep an eye on Mother.

That was the only good thing about it.

Day after day, hour after hour, I stood at an assembly line, churning out screws. I hated every second of it. A trained ape could have done the work just as well, if it were stupid enough to be bullied into submission. The monotony was soul-crushing, the hours long, the factory air thick with the metallic scent of oil and sweat. The machines clanked and whirred, a relentless, deafening rhythm that drummed its way into my skull.

But worse than the physical exhaustion was the knowledge that I was aiding the Nazi war machine. With every screw I manufactured, I was helping to build weapons that would kill more people, prolong the war, and deepen the suffering. It made my stomach turn.

I worked sixty hours a week. By the time I stumbled home in the evenings, my hands raw and my limbs aching, I had no energy for anything else. The thought of Munich, of the *White Rose*, of the work Hans and I had started, felt like a dream slipping through my fingers.

I had only one means of rebellion. *Passive resistance. Sabotage.*

Now, at last, I had the chance to practice exactly what we had urged others to do in our leaflets.

I slowed my pace, deliberately reducing my output to half of what it should have been.

'Sophie Scholl, you are too slow! Can't you see you're holding up the entire line?'

The foreman's voice cracked like a whip over the clatter of machinery. He was a hard-eyed, thick-necked man who thrived on intimidation, no doubt under pressure from his own superiors to squeeze every last ounce of production from us.

I met his glare and shrugged. 'I'm just clumsy,' I said, feigning helplessness. 'I can't help it.'

He muttered something under his breath and moved on, already looking for his next victim.

I caught the eye of the Russian woman beside me. *Nina*. She had been watching the exchange with quiet amusement, a ghost of a smile on her lips.

Nina didn't understand German, but she had a childlike faith in people. She seemed to find the German overseers comical rather than frightening, though I couldn't understand how. I whispered to her in the little Russian I had picked up from Alex. Her face lit up.

I had been horrified to discover just how many Russian women and girls worked in the factory. Forced labourers, torn from their homes, crammed into barracks behind barbed wire, treated as less than human. Their workweeks stretched to seventy hours. They were so thin, their faces pale and drawn, their hands trembling from exhaustion. Their rations were barely enough to keep them alive – thin, watery soup and a scrap of stale bread if they were lucky.

At first, they regarded me with suspicion. A German girl, clean and well-fed, from a good family. I couldn't blame them for keeping their distance.

But I smiled whenever I caught their eyes, wanting them to know that I was not their enemy. Slowly, their wariness faded. They began nodding when I attempted Russian phrases, giggling at my awkward pronunciation.

And when the foreman wasn't looking, I smuggled them pieces of bread, slipping them into their hands beneath the cover of the worktable.

They never said a word.

But their fingers closed tightly around the food, their gratitude shining in their eyes.

Russia was never far from my mind. Almost everyone I loved was there or soon would be. My younger brother, Werner, was somewhere on the Eastern Front. Hans, Alex, and Willi were on their way. And Fritz – recently promoted to Captain, though he was uneasy about the title – would soon be headed for Stalingrad. He was beginning to question the fine line between obeying orders and following one's conscience. I had hoped, perhaps naively, that he might be granted leave to visit before the new term started. But he told me not to count on it. The Russian campaign would stretch on until winter, at least. Some units had been out there since June of the previous year. Still, he hoped for a miracle.

Hans wrote a long letter from Warsaw, where they had stopped for a few days. He described the journey through Germany and Poland as almost idyllic – hours spent gazing out of the train window, watching thatched farmhouses nestled in birch woods, silver moonlight glowing over the fields. He spared a thought for the Polish prisoners in Germany and understood why they loved their country.

But the Warsaw Ghetto shattered whatever reverie the landscape had conjured. He wrote of a city in ruins, of half-starved children crying for bread in the streets while jazz music blared from nearby cafés. Peasants knelt to kiss the flagstones in churches while just beyond the walls, Jews were herded through the ghetto, crammed into cattle trucks at the Umschlagplatz. 'The mood is doom-laden,' he wrote. And yet, he believed in the inexhaustible strength of the Polish people.

The next letter came from Russia.

'He's seen Werner!' Mother's voice trembled with emotion as she passed me the letter across the table. She had been growing stronger, but the strain of having both her sons on the Eastern Front weighed heavily on her.

I devoured every word.

By sheer chance, Hans and Werner were stationed only a few miles apart and had managed to visit each other. One evening, they took a long walk and ended up at a farmhouse, where they drank vodka and sang Russian songs. Hans had a way of disarming people, even those who had every reason to hate him.

His letters made it sound almost peaceful – long walks, idle hours in the dugout, more like a camping trip than a war. But the undercurrents of danger were ever present. He mentioned rumours of a major Russian offensive. Partisans struck at German supply lines, destroying forty-eight trains in a single week. The German army had flattened entire towns in retaliation. Vyazma was nearly razed to the ground. In Gzhatsk, west of Moscow, the Wehrmacht was mired in mud, their progress slowed to a crawl.

What struck me most was how deeply Hans had fallen in love with Russia, just as Alex had always hoped he would. He described the vastness of the steppes, the endless sky, the luminous white nights. He found the people warm and full of soul, their hatred of Bolshevism an unspoken common ground. In Alex's company, he was welcomed into homes that would have otherwise been closed to him. He attended a Russian Orthodox service and was moved by the singing, by the way the voices of the congregation seemed to rise and vibrate as one. He wrote to me about Dostoyevsky, about *Crime and Punishment*, about how the ideas of good, evil, and freedom took on new meaning when surrounded by the casualties of war. By day, he tended to the wounded; by night, he lost himself in Russian hospitality.

I counted down the days until Hans, Alex, and Willi would return.

That summer, I tore a page from my notebook – the page where I had poured out my love for Alex in a moment of reckless vulnerability. But then I hesitated. *Why should I erase him from my heart?* Instead, I placed the page back, whispering a silent prayer that God would give Alex his rightful place in my heart.

Some people believed we were living in the last days, that the war would end in fire and ruin. Perhaps they were right. But I believed then – as I do now – that none of us ever truly knows how much time we have. A bomb, a stray bullet, a train accident – we are always closer to death than we think. I resolved that if my time came, I would be ready to stand before God.

And then, one night, I had the strangest dream.

Hans and Alex were walking beside me, one on each side. Every few steps, they would lift me off the ground, swinging me through the air like a child. I laughed, weightless and free.

In the dream, Hans turned to me, his face full of certainty. 'I can prove the existence of God,' he said.

'How?' I asked.

'Humans need air to breathe,' he explained. 'And if we only ever exhaled, the whole sky would become stale and polluted. We would suffocate. So God breathes into our world, renewing the air, making it fresh again.'

Then Hans inhaled deeply and exhaled a bright blue stream of air. It rose into the sky, growing larger and larger, chasing away the thick grey clouds. Above us, the heavens turned a brilliant, unbroken blue.

It was so beautiful.

Fritz wrote from Ukraine, his letters carrying the weight of everything he had witnessed – the trials, the dangers, the relentless grind of war.

As part of a routine Signal Corps operation, he had flown to a command post close to the front lines. Navigating by poor-quality German maps and relying on indistinct landmarks in the vast, feature-less terrain, their navigator lost his bearings. The mistake was nearly fatal. They had drifted into Russian-held territory, far beyond the safety of German lines. Had it not been for sheer luck – or perhaps fate – they would have been shot down. By some miracle, the Russians below were in the process of surrendering to German forces at that very moment. 'It could have been bad,' Fritz wrote with characteristic understatement, as if he were describing an unfortunate delay rather than a near brush with death.

As dusk fell, the pilot turned the plane back toward safer skies, but finding a place to land near their troops proved impossible. The fighting was too intense, the land torn apart by trenches, shell holes, and scattered wreckage. Eventually, with fuel running low, they were forced to land in an empty field in the middle of nowhere.

They had no weapons. No blankets. The night air cut through them like ice. They dared not light a fire – one flicker of flame, and they would become an easy target.

Fritz lay awake on the frozen ground, staring up at the endless sky, his body stiff with cold. Flares lit up the horizon, illuminating the wreckage of war in eerie, flickering light. Nearby, machine-gun fire rattled without pause, a sound so constant it became part of the landscape.

Hour after hour, millions of soldiers think of nothing except killing each other. Families are torn apart and plunged into deep sorrow.

The destruction was mindless. The Germans were not merely defeating their enemy – they were obliterating everything in their wake. Entire villages were reduced to ruins. Cattle were slaughtered, vegetable plots uprooted. The fields were left barren, stripped of any chance for survival. Nothing remained for the local population but starvation.

But it was the suffering of prisoners that haunted him the most.

On a stretch of road, he came across a group of about twenty Russian soldiers – prisoners of war. Except they were no longer prisoners. They were corpses, sprawled in the dirt where they had fallen. Exhausted, starved, too weak to continue, they had collapsed on the roadside. Their German guards had shot them where they lay.

There were no words for the horror of it.

Reading his letter, my hands trembled with fury and grief.

I could not sit idly by in Ulm any longer. I longed to be back in Munich, to resume our resistance work with the *White Rose*. The Nazis had to be stopped. No matter the risk, no matter the cost.

Chapter
Twenty-Three

February 1943

I open my eyes to find Else watching me, her face drawn, her eyes shadowed with exhaustion. The light above us has burned all night.

She hasn't slept.

Guilt prickles at me. I've stolen her rest, yet she's still here, keeping watch as if she's my guardian angel.

'Did you sleep well, Sophie?' she asks softly.

I stretch, shaking off the stiffness in my limbs. 'I did, actually.'

Else smiles, but it doesn't reach her tired eyes.

'Do you know,' I continue, 'I had the most amazing dream.'

She leans forward, urging me on. 'Tell me about it.'

The images remain sharp, vivid, as though they are something I have truly lived.

'I was carrying a child – a baby, really – wrapped in a long white Christening gown. I was climbing a steep mountain, holding the baby tightly to keep her safe. The church where she was to be baptised was at the very top. But just as I was nearing it, a vast crevasse opened in front of me. A great, yawning abyss.'

Else's eyes widen in horror.

'I had only a moment,' I go on, 'just enough time to set the child down safely – before I fell.'

I pause. The import of the dream settles on my shoulders, though I feel no fear.

Else presses a hand to her mouth. 'That sounds terrifying.'

'Only for a moment,' I assure her. 'But I think I understand what it means.'

She waits.

'The child is not a child at all – it's an idea. *Our* idea. The White Rose. And it will live on, even if we don't. Even if we fall into the abyss, the idea will be carried forward. Others will take it up. Others will climb that mountain in our place.'

Tears shimmer in Else's eyes. Without a word, she steps forward and takes me in her arms, holding me so tightly it's as if she can keep me here, hold me in the world a little longer.

Her voice is barely a whisper. 'If anything happens to you, Sophie, I swear I'll tell your parents about our time together. About your courage. About your light.'

I squeeze her hand. 'God be with you, Else.'

We hear the sound of boots in the corridor. The key turns in the lock.

The guards have come for me.

Chapter Twenty-Four

October 1942

I n mid-October, a letter arrived from Hans.

'He'll be home in a couple of weeks,' Mother said, exhaling a long, weary sigh. Relief softened her face for the first time in months. The strain of worry – Hans and Werner in Russia, Father in prison – had etched new lines into her features. She passed me the letter with trembling fingers.

I scanned the page quickly, my heart hammering.

Nothing could be more important than rejoining you.

He reassured us that Werner was in good hands and that the Russian shelling of Gzhatsk had stopped.

I wasn't sure what to make of the situation on the Eastern Front. Fritz's letters painted a different picture from the newspapers, filled with contradictions and vague optimism. One thing was clear: Hitler had shifted his focus south, toward the Volga. His next target was Stalingrad.

Hans was coming home, but Fritz was not. Neither was Werner.

Russia had seeped into Hans's soul. His letters brimmed with descriptions so vivid, I felt as if I could see it through his eyes – the sudden descent of night over the vast, empty plains, the leaves turning yellow, the birch trees shivering like young girls in the cold. The thin frost on the ground was:

Nature's mourning garb. Death makes life precious.

But their time there had not been easy.

Alex had fallen ill. Diphtheria. A raging fever. My heart clenched as I read the words. How close had he come to death? Hans hadn't said. I prayed desperately for his recovery, as if my pleas could reach across the miles to where he lay burning up with sickness.

My prayers were answered.

Hans wrote that Alex was recovering, though his spirits were low. He didn't want to leave Russia. He longed to stay.

And I – foolish, lovesick – I dreaded the thought that he might not return.

Fritz continued to write, but as winter tightened its grip, his letters became less frequent. He was overwhelmed with work, unable to put pen to paper for nine days.

Then, in the space of two days, two letters arrived.

So that we do not lose one another.

Their mess hall was being closed, forcing them to share facilities with other companies. His most intelligent officer – one of the few men he could truly talk to – was going on study leave. The first snowfall had begun to settle over the landscape, blanketing everything in a deceptive quiet.

He asked me to send him a recorder and an instruction book.

> *I long for music. Something to break the monotony of these endless nights. If I can't listen to it, I will learn to make it myself.*

I sent the recorder and wrote to him about an air raid in Munich. It was foolish of me – I should have known how he'd react. His next letter arrived full of concern.

> *Be very careful. Go to the air raid shelter in plenty of time. Promise me you will.*

But it was his last warning that chilled me the most.

> *I fear the war could turn gruesome very quickly. Gas warfare...*

He didn't elaborate, but the implication was clear. He had seen reports – perhaps overheard rumours – of breaches in the Geneva Convention.

I suspected that if anyone was ignoring the Convention's rules on the treatment of prisoners, it wasn't the Allies.

It was us.

Alex did not get his wish to remain in Russia. He returned with Hans and the others in early November. After reporting to their barracks, Hans and Alex came straight to Ulm to spend a few days with us before the new term began. We were overjoyed to see them.

Yet the moment they stepped through the door, I knew they had changed.

Hans carried himself differently – more serious, more restrained, as though weighed down by something he wasn't ready to share. Alex, once full of restless energy, had grown gaunt. His illness had hollowed out his cheeks and left his eyes sunken with exhaustion. Even their silences felt different. I longed to ask about Russia, about everything they had seen, but instinct told me to wait. Just as Hans had needed time to process Nuremberg – what now felt like a lifetime ago – so he would need time to process Russia.

The other good news was that Father was home. Released from prison two months early, he walked through the front door looking thinner but utterly unrepentant. Prison had not broken his spirit – if anything, it had only hardened his resolve.

At dinner that first evening, he sat at the head of the table, raising his glass as if nothing had changed. 'Remember,' he declared, his voice as steady as ever, 'stand tall against all forces, and survive!'

As if we needed reminding.

I caught Hans's eye across the table. He was already thinking ahead, eager to return to Munich and restart our *White Rose* activities.

I couldn't wait.

The new term commenced in November.

This time, Hans and I rented two rooms in an apartment on Franz-Joseph Strasse, just a short walk from the university. Our land-lady, Frau Schmidt, spent most of her time in the countryside with her sister to avoid the bombing raids. Her frequent absences were a gift. We could have friends over whenever we pleased, and more importantly, we could resume the work of the *White Rose* without interference.

Despite the end of her relationship with Hans, Traute remained committed to helping us print and distribute leaflets. Hans was now seeing my friend Gisela Schertling, but she knew nothing of our ac-tivities. That was how tightly we guarded our circle. Either you were on the inside, or you weren't.

Christoph Probst had transferred to Innsbruck with a Luftwaffe medical unit, so we rarely saw him. But Alex and Willi were always around, practically living in our apartment.

Through foreign radio broadcasts, we learned of other resis-tance groups. That was how we heard about the arrests of Harro Schulze-Boysen and Arvid Harnack in Berlin in August and September. They belonged to *Die Rote Kapelle* – The Red Orchestra – an anti-Nazi resistance network operating in the capital. We weren't alone.

Hans was electrified by the news. 'We have to connect with them,' he insisted. 'We have to expand.'

But how? Making contact with another resistance cell was perilous.

'Leave it with me,' said Alex.

Through his artist friend Lilo Ramdohr, Alex arranged a meeting with Falk Harnack, the brother of Arvid Harnack. Falk was involved in the underground movement and could help us make the right connections.

'We'll have to take a train to Chemnitz, near the Czech border,' Alex told Hans when the plans were finalized.

Hans nodded. 'Fine.'

'You don't have a travel permit,' I pointed out. 'Neither does Alex.' The Gestapo was tightening its grip on rail travel, especially near border regions. Being caught without proper documentation could mean prison – or worse. 'You could be charged with desertion.'

'We're going,' said Hans. His tone left no room for argument.

The day they left for Chemnitz, I found it impossible to concentrate. Every hour that passed felt like a weight pressing down on my chest. One mistake, one careless word, and everything we had worked for could be undone.

When I heard footsteps in the hallway that evening, I rushed to the door.

'You're back!'

'Of course we're back,' said Alex, pulling off his gloves, his usual nonchalance grating on my nerves.

'How did it go?'

Hans set down his rucksack and stretched. 'Good.'

'I want to hear everything.'

'Any chance of some tea first? I'm parched.'

Hans had brought back a beautiful brass samovar from Russia, which now sat proudly on a chest of drawers. I busied myself making tea, my impatience barely contained.

At last, we sat down.

'Falk was encouraging,' Hans began. 'He said there's a broad resistance movement stretching from the military on the right to the Communists on the left.'

I sat forward. 'And?'

'He asked how we felt about working with Communists.'

'And what did you say?'

'We told him we have no issue with it. Right now, the priority is overthrowing National Socialism. If that means working with Communists, so be it.'

I nodded. Ideological differences meant nothing in the face of tyranny.

'What about the military?' I asked. 'They're the only ones with the power to remove Hitler.'

Hans hesitated, then said, 'Falk couldn't give specifics. But he did say something interesting. There's a group planning to assassinate Hitler and overthrow the government.'

I stared at him. 'Are you serious?'

He nodded.

'Then why haven't they done it already?' The words tumbled out before I could stop them.

Hans gave a small, grim smile. 'That's the question, isn't it?'

For a moment, none of us spoke. The mere thought of Hitler's death was intoxicating. If it was true – if there really were people plotting inside the military – then perhaps the nightmare *could* end.

'So what happens now?' I asked.

'We told Falk we want to join forces with the Berlin resistance,' Hans said. 'He's going to arrange a meeting soon.'

A thrill ran through me. This was the moment we had been waiting for. Travelling to Chemnitz had been worth the risk.

The real fight was just beginning.

Chapter Twenty-Five

February 1943

The guards march me down the corridor, the heavy tread of their boots echoing against the bare walls. My heart pounds. They do not say where they are taking me. Then, the door opens, and I see Hans.

I rush into his arms. For a fleeting moment, I feel the warmth of his embrace, the strength that has always been there. But the guards tear us apart, yanking me back. Even this small act is forbidden.

I step back and look at him properly. He has lost weight, his face pale, his eyes shadowed – but he stands tall, unbroken.

Christoph is there too, looking lost, his face drawn with sorrow. I reach out my hand to him. He hesitates, then grips it, just for a moment, before offering a flicker of a smile.

Footsteps in the corridor. Voices.

The door opens again. Herr Mohr enters, carrying a sheaf of papers and pens. He lays three sets of paper before us.

'I advise all of you to write farewell letters to your families,' he says, his voice level. 'There won't be time after the trial.'

The words hit me like a slap.

Won't be time? Not even to write a letter?

It is a foregone conclusion. The verdict has already been decided. The trial will be nothing but a performance, a grotesque parody of justice.

I sit, my hands trembling as I pick up a pen. Across from me, Hans and Christoph begin writing immediately, as if sitting an exam and racing against the clock. Hans, always quick with words, is scribbling furiously, his head bent over the paper.

I stare at the blank sheet before me.

How do you write the last letter of your life?

I, who have written hundreds of letters, who have filled the pages of my diary with thoughts, now falter. How can I express everything I feel?

I inhale sharply and begin.

> *Dear Mother and Father,*
> *Thank you for all the goodness and love you have given me. Please forgive me for the pain I am now causing you. Please understand that I did what I felt was right and could not have acted otherwise.*
> *My greatest concern is for Mother, whose health is so fragile. I know this will break her heart. But I believe Father will understand. He has always told us to stand tall against all forces. And that is what I have done.*

'Two minutes,' Mohr says.

Two minutes. For a lifetime of love and farewells.

I sign my name hurriedly, then grab another sheet.

Dearest Inge,
Tell Carl Muth... tell him I carried his words with me
until the end. Stand strong. Be happy. Live.

I fold it and reach for one last page. Fritz.

What can I say to him? I want to tell him everything – that he filled my life with light, that he is in my thoughts even now, that I hope he will live on and find happiness, even without me.

Instead, I write only what I can fit into the time I have left.

My dearest Fritz,
You brought such joy into my life. Don't forget me. Be
happy.

'Stop,' Mohr orders.

I lower my pen. It is done.

He gathers up our letters and mumbles something about ensuring they reach their recipients. I do not believe him. I do not believe a word the Gestapo says. But what else can I do?

The guards step forward. Hans, Christoph, and I exchange one last look before we are separated.

Outside, two unmarked cars wait, engines idling. I am led to the first car. The door slams shut behind me. Hans and Christoph are taken to the second car. Another slam. Another lock turned. Then, the cars pull away.

And we are driven toward our fate.

Chapter Twenty-Six

November –
December 1942

The meeting with Falk Harnack gave Hans renewed confidence. We needed to expand. Our words had to travel beyond Munich, beyond Bavaria – we had to reach every corner of the Reich. Only then could we hope to make a real impact.

'We have to build a network,' Hans told us. 'We can't do this alone.'

His energy was infectious. We made plans, each more ambitious than the last.

Hans put me in charge of finances. The weeks I had spent helping in Father's office proved to be useful training. I recorded every mark spent, every sheet of paper bought, every envelope and postage stamp that left our possession. We were running a resistance movement, but I treated it with the precision of a business – because any misstep could mean disaster.

Funding our cause was the next challenge.

Hans and Alex travelled to Stuttgart to meet with Father's old friend, Eugen Grimminger. Instead of risking conversation indoors, they walked the streets, talking in low voices to avoid being overheard. Hans laid out our plans – the leaflets, the expansion, the goal of igniting something larger.

Herr Grimminger listened carefully, his expression unreadable. Then, after a moment of silence, he said, 'I will think it over.'

A short time later, we received a cheque for 500 Reichsmarks.

I noted it in our accounts, my hands trembling slightly as I wrote down the figure. That would buy a lot of stationery. It would also, I knew, increase the stakes. Grimminger was taking a risk by supporting us. We could not afford to fail.

Meanwhile, Traute travelled to Hamburg with leaflets hidden in her luggage. There, she met with a handful of trusted friends, slipping the folded pages into their hands.

'They were eager to help,' she reported back. 'They want to distribute the leaflets themselves.'

And just like that, the *White Rose* had its first branch outside Munich.

Back in Munich, Hans befriended a bookshop owner named Josef Söhngen. His shop, in Maximilianplatz, was more than a place to buy books – it was a sanctuary for forbidden ideas. He stocked works by Franz Kafka, Thomas Mann, Stefan Zweig – books the Nazis had banned, books people whispered about but rarely dared to own. Josef knew the risks. And yet, he took them anyway.

But the person Hans and Alex truly wanted to recruit was Professor Kurt Huber.

They arranged a visit to his home in Gräfelfing. When they arrived, Professor Huber led them to his study, closing the door behind him to keep out the sounds of his young children. He gestured for them to sit.

Hans wasted no time. He revealed that he and Alex were the authors of the *White Rose* leaflets.

The professor's eyebrows shot up. For a long moment, he said nothing. Then, he exhaled sharply. 'Well,' he said finally, 'I should have guessed.'

He was intrigued, but sceptical. As he had at the Schmorells' house, he questioned the effectiveness of the leaflets.

'Words alone are not enough,' he said. 'We need more drastic action. Without blood, it won't work. The Wehrmacht is the only force capable of destroying the Nazis.'

Hans leaned forward. 'We have contacts in Berlin,' he said carefully. 'We know people within the military. A reliable source has told us there are plans to kill Hitler.'

Professor Huber nearly fell off his chair. 'You're serious?'

Hans nodded.

Silence stretched between them. Then, slowly, the professor sat back, steepling his fingers. The flicker of hesitation in his eyes faded, replaced by something else.

Resolve.

'I will support you,' he said.

Hans and Alex exchanged glances. This was it. The *White Rose* was no longer just a handful of students printing leaflets in the shadows. We were growing. And for the first time, it felt like we had a real chance of making a difference.

I didn't hear from Fritz from mid-November until early December. When his letter finally arrived, my hands trembled as I unfolded the thin sheet of paper. He was still alive – and that was no longer something to take for granted.

The Russians had forced the Germans to abandon their airport. His unit had fought their way to the east bank of the Don River, losing vehicles, equipment, and many men in the process. He was no longer working in intelligence. His Signal Corps unit had been transformed into an infantry battalion, defending a crumbling sector. The weight of life-and-death decisions now rested on his shoulders.

'You should listen to the news,' he wrote, 'so you can understand what we are facing.'

What he didn't realise was that the German news reports told us nothing. The Eastern Front was an abyss, its truth swallowed by propaganda. If I wanted to know what was really happening, I had only his letters to rely on. I devoured every word – not just for his personal news but for the unvarnished glimpse they gave me into the war.

Yet even amid the horror, there were fleeting moments of beauty. Under relentless Russian bombardment, a small bird had appeared on the edge of his foxhole, singing as if the war didn't exist. He took it as a sign – a greeting from me, a reminder of life beyond the battlefield. For a moment, he felt safe, as if nothing could touch him.

But safety was an illusion. He was trapped in what he called the 'Stalingrad Cauldron,' a name that sent shivers down my spine. He described the eerie quiet that would suddenly give way to the relentless chatter of machine-gun fire. The Russians were just 300 metres away.

And yet, he told me, death was not what he feared most.

> *What I fear, is becoming indifferent to it. That I will stop seeing the enemy as human. That killing will no longer feel like a terrible thing.*

His words burned in my mind long after I put down his letter.

He apologized that he wouldn't be able to send me a Christmas present this year. The only gift he could offer was his words.

> *Prayer is my foothold in all the frenzy. And I pray for you, Sophie.*

I pressed the letter to my chest, murmuring a silent prayer of my own.

On the last night of term, we gathered in our apartment – Hans, Alex, Willi, and me. The air smelled of candle wax and the faint, lingering scent of the cognac Hans had just uncorked. He poured generous measures into glasses while I made tea. Outside, the winter wind howled through the streets of Munich, rattling the windowpanes.

As always, our conversation turned to the resistance.

'We need to go further,' I said, leaning forward, my fingers wrapped around my teacup for warmth. 'Leaflets aren't enough. What about a graffiti campaign?'

Hans raised his eyebrows, intrigued. 'Graffiti?'

I nodded. 'So many good people are risking their lives in this senseless war, but hardly anyone is willing to risk their life fighting evil. Someone has to do it.'

Willi tapped his fingers on the arm of his chair, thinking. 'It's dangerous,' he admitted. 'But I like it.'

'Dangerous,' Alex echoed, stretching his long legs in front of him and lighting his pipe. He exhaled a plume of smoke into the air, his sharp features thoughtful. Then a slow grin spread across his face. 'That's what makes it effective.'

'We can't afford to be slow,' said Hans, his excitement growing. 'We'd need to work fast.'

Alex, ever the artist, sat up straighter. 'Then we use stencils.'

Hans looked at him, intrigued. 'Stencils?'

'Yes. One person holds the stencil against the wall, another paints, and the third keeps watch. It'll be quicker, cleaner, and more striking.' His eyes gleamed. 'We can make them huge.'

I could already picture it – bold, defiant words scrawled across Nazi buildings, on the walls of the university, where no one could ignore them. A message no propaganda machine could erase.

Hans, a born risk-taker, was already scribbling a list. 'We'll need paint, brushes.'

'And courage,' Willi added dryly.

'That,' said Hans, lifting his glass, 'we have in abundance.'

We clinked our glasses together. The fire crackled in the hearth, casting long shadows on the walls. The city outside was silent, but inside our small apartment, rebellion was alive.

Before we knew it, Christmas was upon us.

Fritz wrote the day before Christmas Eve. His letter was brief, but its words weighed heavily. He would be spending Christmas on the battlefield.

The situation had worsened. His battalion had been reassigned to a new sector, one that was under relentless attack.

The earth shakes and seethes all day under artillery fire.
Losses are mounting.

He admitted that he had begun to detach himself from reality. The fear of death no longer haunted him as it once had.

What is the point in dreading the inevitable?

It was unbearable to read such words from Fritz. In my mind, I could see him crouched in a freezing trench, surrounded by the endless white void of a Russian winter, shells pounding the ground around him. How much longer could he endure?

In Ulm, our Christmas celebrations unfolded as they always had – candles flickered on the tree, the scent of pine and cinnamon filled the house, we exchanged presents. But the warmth and familiarity of home could not shield us from reality. Werner was still in Russia. And Hans and I could think of nothing but our plans for the *White Rose*.

On Christmas morning, Hans invited Inge for a walk. When he returned, he found me in the kitchen, where the glow from the stove barely touched the cold creeping in from the windows.

'She doesn't understand,' he said.

He poured himself a cup of tea and sat down at the table, his gaze fixed on some distant point beyond the walls of our home.

'What did you talk about?' I asked, though I already sensed his disappointment.

'I told her about the places I want to see – Egypt, China, the open ocean stretching beyond the horizon.' He gave a small, wistful smile. 'People should have something to look forward to, Sophie. The future *should* be more than war and rubble.'

I nodded, waiting for him to go on.

'But it's not just that,' he said, his fingers tightening around the cup. 'People need to know what a post-Nazi world will look like. If we want people to resist, to believe in change, we have to show them an alternative. A government based on justice. A future worth fighting for.'

I could see how much this mattered to him. It wasn't just about opposing Hitler anymore; it was about what came after. He wanted to rebuild, not just destroy.

'What did Inge say?'

His jaw clenched. 'She told me not to do anything reckless. She reminded me that Father has already paid the price for speaking out. That he was arrested, imprisoned, disbarred, and now has to scrape by with bookkeeping jobs.' He exhaled sharply. 'She told me to think of *them*.'

'And what did you say?'

'I told her that *someone* has to take action. That we can't just wait for the war to end and hope everything falls into place. Communists can't be the only ones to hold their heads high after the defeat of Nazism.' He sighed, rubbing his temple. 'She didn't want to hear it.'

For a moment, we sat in silence. The fire crackled softly in the hearth. Outside, a light dusting of snow had settled over Ulm, the streets quiet under the weight of winter.

'She's afraid,' I said at last.

Hans nodded. 'I know.' He set down his cup and straightened his shoulders. 'But fear won't change anything.'

Among the Scholls, Hans and I were on our own.

We returned to Munich in early January. Classes had yet to resume, giving us time to reconnect with our friends. When Alex and Willi dropped by the apartment on Franz-Joseph Strasse, tea and talk flowed in equal measure.

Manfred Eickemeyer was back on leave from Kraków and invited us to his studio. The moment we stepped inside, we knew this would not be a social call. His face was grave, his voice low. He told us everything.

The extermination camps. The gassings.

Hearing such things spoken aloud, not as rumours but as facts, made my stomach churn. How could such horror exist? The words pressed against my ribs like iron bars.

'If God is omnipotent,' I asked aloud, 'why does He not intervene? How can His power be reconciled with human free will?'

Manfred had no answers. None of us did. But our resolve hardened. There was no turning back now. We had to do more.

It was time to write the fifth leaflet.

> *A Call to All Germans!*
> *The war is nearing its inevitable end... Hitler cannot*
> *win the war, only prolong it.*

With a wider network in place, we now dared to address all Germans. We wanted our words to reach beyond Munich, beyond the universities, to every citizen of the Reich.

Falk Harnack had urged us to be more direct, less literary. This time, there were no quotes from Schiller or Goethe. No poetry. Just facts and a warning.

Are we to be forever the nation hated and rejected by all mankind?

We looked beyond resistance and toward the future. What would Germany become when Hitler was gone?

Prussian militarism must never come to power again... The coming Germany must be federalist... Freedom of speech, freedom of religion, the protection of the individual citizen from the arbitrary will of criminal regimes – these will be the foundations of the New Europe.

How optimistic we were. In January 1943 – just one month ago! – we truly believed the Allied invasion was imminent. That the tide was turning. That German citizens, if given the right push, might finally wake up.

Hans and Alex gave a draft to Professor Huber and asked for his input.

He did not go easy on them.

Alex, he thought, was far too sympathetic to the Soviet Union. Huber despised Communism. He hated Hitler, but he revered the German military, the old Prussian ideals of discipline and honour. To him, the enemy was not the soldiers dying on the battlefield but the corrupt regime that had sent them there.

Hans had deliberately omitted *The White Rose* from this leaflet. Professor Huber disagreed. 'The *White Rose*,' he insisted, 'stands for purity and courage.'

But Hans wanted to be taken more seriously. We were no longer a few university students. We were *a movement.* The leaflet was titled: *Leaflets of the Resistance.*

While Hans, Alex, and Huber wrangled over wording, Traute and I had our own work to do. We spent days visiting shops all over Munich, buying paper, envelopes, and stamps – never in large enough quantities to arouse suspicion.

Alex purchased a new typewriter and a larger duplicating machine, both hidden in the basement of Eickemeyer's studio. At last, the final draft was approved.

Production began.

Night after night, we laboured, the rhythmic crank of the mimeograph machine filling the air. The ink smudged our fingers, our arms ached, our nerves frayed. Stencils broke and had to be replaced. Sleep became a luxury we could no longer afford. Fear, however, we could not escape. The Gestapo had eyes and ears everywhere. If they caught us, we knew what awaited us.

Hans was struggling under the weight of it all. He would walk past friends in the street without seeing them, convinced he was being followed. I lived in a constant state of tension, appearing outwardly cheerful while a kind of emotional paralysis crept over me in my solitude.

As if the fear of discovery weren't enough, the RAF had begun bombing Munich more frequently. Each air raid threatened to expose us. If Eickemeyer's studio were destroyed, someone would eventually ask: *What was an architect doing with a duplicating machine?*

Hans devised a contingency plan.

If an air raid siren sounded, he would call the bookseller, Josef Söhngen, and ask if he had a certain book in stock. If Söhngen replied yes, the coast was clear. Hans and Alex would then haul the duplicating machine through the blacked-out streets and store it in the bookshop's cellar. A duplicating machine in a bookshop was far easier to explain.

At last, we had thousands of leaflets ready.

This time, we would not limit ourselves to Munich. We had addresses for cities all over Germany – Berlin, Cologne, Hamburg. And the letters would not all be posted from one place.

Hans was to travel to Salzburg. Alex to Linz and Vienna.

I would go to Augsburg, Ulm, and Stuttgart.

I packed a rucksack with leaflets and set off for the station alone. Just another young woman travelling to visit a friend. Nothing for the Gestapo to notice.

But my heart pounded all the same. Plainclothes officers patrolled the platforms, watching, listening. They were searching for deserters, for smugglers, for anyone out of place.

I bought my ticket, boarded the train, and found an empty compartment. Without hesitation, I placed my rucksack in the overhead rack and stepped back into the corridor, looking for another seat elsewhere.

A family entered the compartment I had just vacated. Good. The rucksack would not be traced to me if something went wrong.

I found another half-occupied compartment. The man opposite me smoked a pipe. A woman knitted in silence. No one spoke. People no longer made conversation with strangers.

I forced myself to relax.

The train was late. Nothing ran on time anymore. Half an hour became an hour. Two.

When the police finally came to check papers, I forced myself to meet their gaze with steady confidence. They handed mine back without a second glance.

When we arrived in Augsburg, I waited until the platform had mostly emptied before retrieving the rucksack. If it had been discovered, the train would have been stopped, passengers questioned.

Outside, the streets were dark and empty. My breath curled in the frozen air. I needed postboxes. Quiet streets. No witnesses. I reached a deserted corner, eased the rucksack off my back, and reached inside.

Then – a low rumble. A car approached. I froze, heart hammering.

A black limousine. Gestapo.

I grabbed the rucksack and melted into the shadows.

The car passed, indifferent. Not stopping. Not slowing.

I waited. Counted to thirty.

Then, as quickly as I could, I stuffed a handful of envelopes into the postbox and moved on.

I roamed the city for hours, finding more postboxes, more dark corners. The leaflets were addressed to homes across Germany. Frankfurt. Cologne. Berlin.

By the time I dropped the last handful, I was exhausted. My body ached from sleepless nights. I made my way back to the train station. The first train to Munich would not leave for hours. I sat on a wooden bench, shivering, waiting for dawn.

It had been a long night. But it had been worth it.

Chapter Twenty-Seven

February 1943

The cars race through the streets of Munich, their engines growling as they cut through the city's broad avenues. Outside, life continues as normal – people walking to work, a cyclist weaving between trams, a mother pulling her child's hand as they cross the road. I watch them through the window, each step they take widening the gulf between their reality and mine.

Less than ten minutes later, we swerve to a stop outside the Palace of Justice on Prielmayerstrasse.

The doors are yanked open.

A guard drags me from the car, his grip firm on my arm. The cold February air stings my cheeks, but I barely register it before I am pushed forward, forced inside.

They hurry me through the atrium, our feet echoing on the marble floor. Around me I glimpse pillars and arches and, up above, a domed glass roof.

They march me up a grand, sweeping staircase. Then the doors of the courtroom swing open. They shove me inside.

The courtroom is all wood panelling and gloomy portraits in oil of long-dead men. And above the judge's bench – watching, omnipresent – hangs a portrait of Adolf Hitler.

This is the People's Court.

But there will be no justice here.

Hans, Christoph, and I are led to the dock, flanked by policemen. Only when we are seated do I take my first real look around.

The room is packed, standing room only. A sea of brown and black uniforms. SS officers, party officials, and Gestapo agents all jostle for position, eager to witness the spectacle. They turn their faces toward us, their eyes hungry, dissecting us like specimens in a glass case.

Some wear sneers of triumph. Others appear puzzled – perhaps by our youth, perhaps by the sight of a young woman among the accused. *How could three students threaten the mighty Reich?*

I meet their stares, one by one. I will not cower. I will not look away.

I scan the rows of faces, searching. Is anyone here for us? I don't see our parents. Do they know about the trial? The arrest, the investigation, the indictment – everything has moved with terrifying speed. The Gestapo want this trial over before the world has time to take notice.

Then, a murmur ripples through the room. The noise swells, then hushes all at once. Everyone rises.

The door at the back of the courtroom swings open, and a man sweeps in, swathed in scarlet robes. Else told me who would be presiding. Roland Freisler. The president of the People's Court. The man who will decide our fate.

He is taller than I expected, with a sharp, birdlike face and a high, balding forehead. His deep-set, hooded eyes sweep over us, radiating contempt. He does not see three students before him. He sees enemies of the Reich.

Black-robed judges take their seats on either side of him, a flock of crows ready to feast on the scraps.

Freisler slams a file down on his desk. The trial begins. We already know how it will end.

Chapter
Twenty-Eight

January 1943

I n mid-January, an order went out for all students to attend a speech in the Main Auditorium of the Deutsche Museum to mark the 470th anniversary of Munich University. The speaker was Paul Giesler, the Gauleiter of Munich. A Nazi functionary, not an academic.

Hans, Alex, Willi, and I had no intention of going. As members of the *White Rose*, we had vowed to boycott all Nazi events. We advocated passive resistance. We refused to give them our attention, our presence, or our obedience.

Instead, we spent the afternoon in the apartment, drinking tea and debating our next move. It wasn't until later, when Gisela Schertling, and Anneliese Graf, Willi's sister, arrived, that we learned what had happened.

Gisela burst through the door, still breathless from the cold.

'You won't believe it,' she said, peeling off her coat. 'The whole place exploded.'

We stared at her.

'What do you mean?' Hans asked.

Anneliese stepped forward, eyes bright with excitement. 'The speech. It turned into a full-blown protest.'

Hans set down his cup. 'Tell us everything.'

Gisela dropped into a chair. 'The auditorium was packed – not just students and professors. Party officials. Military officers. SS. Swastikas everywhere. Most of us students were crammed into the balcony.'

I could picture it all too well. The red banners hanging from every wall, the sea of brown and black uniforms, the suffocating air of fear and obedience. I was so glad I hadn't gone.

'What did Giesler say?' I asked.

Anneliese rolled her eyes. 'He ranted about how Munich wasn't sending enough sons to the Russian front, that people were too weak, too soft. Then he said the university couldn't remain an "ivory tower" of intellectual thought. That it had to be part of National Socialism.'

'He wouldn't know an intellectual thought if it bit him in the bollocks,' Alex muttered.

We burst out laughing.

'But then,' Gisela continued, lowering her voice, 'he started on the women.'

My laughter died. 'What do you mean?'

Anneliese leaned forward, her face dark. 'He said that university was no place for women. That we were shirking our war duties.'

'What crap,' I snapped, thinking of the long, brutal hours I'd spent in the armaments factory.

Gisela lifted a hand. 'Wait, wait. You haven't heard the best part yet.'

We watched her expectantly.

'He didn't just say women shouldn't be at university. He said we should be at home, with our husbands, making babies for the Führer.'

The room erupted in laughter.

'I beg your pardon?' Alex choked.

Gisela grinned wickedly. 'Oh, it gets worse. He actually said that if any women weren't attractive enough to get a husband, he would lend them one of his adjutants. And that' – she threw up her hands, mimicking Giesler's pompous tone – 'the experience would be glorious!'

For a moment, there was stunned silence.

Then the room exploded – laughter, outrage, disbelief.

Alex shook his head, grinning. 'The man is a cretin.'

Hans, however, didn't laugh. He was watching Gisela and Anneliese closely. 'What happened next?' he asked.

Anneliese's eyes sparkled. 'Well. That's when the students lost it.'

I leaned in, heart pounding.

'Women started shouting him down,' she said. 'Others stormed out – and the SS arrested them on the spot.'

Gisela nodded. 'Then the male students tried to free them. Fights broke out. Pushing, shoving, chaos. People started chanting, singing freedom songs. Then we all linked arms and marched toward the university.'

'And then?' I asked.

Anneliese sighed. 'It didn't last. It fizzled out when we reached Ludwigstrasse. But for a moment, Sophie, it was real. A real protest.'

I exhaled. A small victory. But a victory nonetheless.

Later, when Gisela and Anneliese had left, Hans said, 'Giesler's just done us a huge favour.'

Alex grinned. 'He's shown everyone what Nazism really is.'

'We need to act now,' Hans said. 'While people are angry.'

I nodded fiercely. 'We should print another thousand copies of *A Call to All Germans*. Get them out fast.'

Hans was already on his feet, grabbing a pencil, scribbling a list of supplies.

None of us noticed Christoph standing apart from the group, his expression troubled.

'The terror is still present,' he said quietly. 'More so now than ever before.'

We barely heard him. We were too caught up in the moment. Too certain that we were riding the wave of something bigger than ourselves. Too blind to see what was coming.

The news from Russia was grim.

In mid-January, Fritz wrote that they had been in retreat for eight days straight. Eight days and nights, sleeping in the open, exposed to temperatures of thirty below freezing. No shelter. No respite.

His battalion had been all but wiped out. His hands were frozen – two fingers in danger of being lost to frostbite. He had staggered to a field hospital, hoping for treatment. They turned him away. His injuries, they said, were 'not serious enough.'

But a man could die from cold as easily as a bullet.

At last, a kind officer let Fritz share his warm bunker. He had thought – truly thought – that he was going to die. Or be taken prisoner. But he had not yet given up all hope.

I will pray. For myself, for you, for all our loved ones.

And then, at the bottom of the page, his farewell:

Greet your parents, your brothers and sisters, and my
family. In case I do not make it home.

I shut my eyes, pressing the letter to my chest. I would not believe this was the end. I refused to believe it.

The news from Stalingrad soon became public. After months of bloodshed, the battle was lost. For the first time, Germany was forced to surrender – forced to admit defeat. We had been told that Stalingrad would be the great victory – the moment we crushed Bolshevism. But instead, it had simply crushed thousands of lives.

I sat with Hans, Alex, and Willi, listening to the radio bulletin. A slow drumbeat, then silence. Then another drumbeat. Then Beethoven. The second movement of his Fifth Symphony. Not the music of victory.

The announcer's voice trembled with barely concealed emotion.

The battle for Stalingrad is over. True, with their last
breath, to their oath to the flag, the Sixth Army, under
the inspirational leadership of General Field Marshal
von Paulus, has been defeated. They died so that Ger-
many may live.

I stared at the radio, numb with rage. They died so that Germany may live? No. They died because of Hitler's madness.

We were more convinced than ever – Germany would lose the war. And we deserved to lose.

Professor Huber was enraged. That night, he worked until dawn, penning a furious denunciation of the war, of the regime, of the cowards in Berlin who sent young men to die. It would become our sixth leaflet.

Meanwhile, Hans, Alex, and Willi took to the streets under cover of darkness. Armed with paint and brushes, they launched their graffiti campaign.

In the morning, the words stood out in bold, defiant strokes on university buildings and public squares:

DOWN WITH HITLER.
FREEDOM!

By noon, prisoners of war – mostly women – were forced to scrub the walls clean. But no amount of scrubbing could fully erase the message. The words remained, faint but defiant, for all to see.

And then – a light in the darkness. Fritz was alive. One of the last flights out of Stalingrad had taken him to a field hospital in Stalino. I sat at my desk, clutching the letter, my hands shaking with relief. 'Thank you, God.'

He had made it. At least, for now.

At the end of January, Liesl came to visit.

She took one look at the apartment and frowned. 'Sophie, how can you live like this?'

She surveyed the apartment with thinly veiled horror – dirty crockery piled high in the sink, books and papers scattered across every surface, clothes draped over chairs and trailing onto the floor.

Liesl had always been neat and tidy, the sort of person who ironed her bedsheets and polished her shoes. To her, this chaos must have been unbearable.

I shrugged, trying to sound casual. 'We've been busy.' I couldn't tell her what we had been doing.

Liesl folded her arms. 'Too busy to wash up?'

She sighed, and then – to my great relief – she rolled up her sleeves. 'Never mind, I'll help you clear up.'

It was an offer I couldn't refuse.

Together, we began sorting and tidying, throwing out rubbish, stacking books, and shoving clothes into drawers. As I bent down to clear a pile of papers off the floor, my fingers brushed against something stiff and unfamiliar. A military train pass. For Alex. Destination: Saarbrücken. Alex must have accidentally dropped it. I snapped.

'What the hell is this doing here?!' I shouted, holding up the pass like an incriminating piece of evidence.

Liesl jumped, startled by my outburst. 'Sophie, what's wrong?'

'This shouldn't be lying around!' My voice was sharp, frantic. How could Alex be so careless? A military train pass – right here, in the open? If the Gestapo ever came searching…

Liesl stared at me, completely baffled. 'Sophie, I'm worried about you. This isn't like you. Why are you making such a fuss over a train pass?'

I forced myself to breathe, to calm down. 'It's nothing,' I mumbled, stuffing it into my pocket.

But my reaction had betrayed me. The stress of living a secret life was getting to me more than I realised. Liesl wasn't stupid. She knew something was wrong. She just didn't know what.

That evening, the telephone rang. Hans answered. Liesl and I sat at the table, only hearing one side of the conversation.

'Christoph, where are you?' Hans asked. A pause. 'The station? Why aren't you coming over?' Another pause. Hans's face tightened. 'No, don't go straight back to Innsbruck. You need your friends. You can't bear all that on your own. I insist you drop in. Alex is coming over. We'll see you soon.'

I saw it in Christoph's face as soon as he walked through the door – the exhaustion, the weight of defeat and worry pressing down on him. His wife, Herta, had been dangerously ill with puerperal fever since the birth of their third child, Katja. On top of everything else, it was too much.

Liesl and I made tea, filling cups with something warm, something normal, while Christoph shed his uniform jacket as though it weighed a hundred pounds.

We sat at the table, listening as he spoke about Herta's illness, about the long nights spent worrying, about his new baby daughter.

'Medicine is advancing all the time,' Liesl reassured him gently. 'There's every chance she'll make a full recovery.'

Christoph tried to smile, but his eyes were heavy with doubt.

Liesl gathered up dirty cups and plates and disappeared into the kitchen. The moment she was out of sight, the conversation shifted.

'We haven't just lost the Battle of Stalingrad,' said Hans with grim satisfaction. 'We've lost the war.'

Alex nodded. 'Anyone can see that now.'

Christoph let out a bitter laugh. 'Hitler and his regime must fall, or Germany will be destroyed.' He hesitated. Then, as if making a decision, he reached into his pocket and pulled out a folded sheet of paper. 'I wrote this,' he said, his fingers tightening around it. 'I just needed to get things off my chest.'

Hans took the paper, unfolding it. Blue ink. Handwritten. 'Another leaflet?'

Christoph shrugged. 'Only if you think it's up to scratch. I don't have your gift with words, but if you can use anything from it, you're welcome to it.'

Hans skimmed the text, nodding slowly.

Then, as Liesl re-entered the room, he folded the paper neatly and slid it into his pocket. A simple, casual gesture. He probably forgot it was there. Until we were arrested.

Falk Harnack visited us in Munich at our apartment on Franz-Joseph-Strasse.

He already knew Hans and Alex from their trip to Chemnitz, but this time, he also met me, Willi, and Professor Huber. I was eager to meet him.

Hans introduced us. I shook Falk's hand. His grip was firm, his gaze steady and intense – a man who had already lost so much but remained unshaken.

'I'm sorry about your brother,' I said.

'Thank you,' he replied, his voice low but resolute. 'We fight on.'

I had no doubt that the execution of Arvid Harnack at the hands of the Nazis had only strengthened his resolve.

The mood in the room was unexpectedly upbeat. Falk had good news.

'The resistance movement in Berlin is paying attention to what you're doing here in Munich,' he said. He looked at each of us, one by one, making sure we grasped the significance. 'People are taking the *White Rose* very seriously.'

I glanced at Hans and Alex. Their expressions brightened. Willi, as always, was harder to read, but even he must have felt encouraged. It meant that our efforts weren't in vain.

Alex, ever the optimist, grinned. 'We're creating a revolutionary atmosphere here in Munich.'

Hans leaned forward, his hands clasped. 'The Allied invasion can't be far off now. We mustn't lose momentum.'

Professor Huber cleared his throat, the familiar signal that he was about to speak. We waited patiently as he gathered himself.

'I've drafted a new leaflet for you to use,' he said. 'I wrote it after the defeat at Stalingrad.'

He pulled several typewritten pages from his briefcase and handed them to Hans.

Hans scanned the first lines, then read aloud: '"Our people are deeply shaken by the fall of our men at Stalingrad. Three hundred and thirty thousand German men were senselessly and irresponsibly driven to their deaths by the brilliant strategy of our World War I corporal. Führer, we thank you!"'

A beat of silence – then Alex burst out laughing, clapping his hands. 'Bravo, Professor!'

A few months ago, Professor Huber had been hesitant, unwilling to fully commit. But now, he had thrown himself into the cause with conviction.

Hans thanked Professor Huber and set the leaflet aside for now. The conversation turned to the wider resistance movement.

'If you want to work with us,' Falk said, 'you'll have to accept that we operate as a broad coalition. We cover the entire political spectrum – from left to right.'

Professor Huber's brow furrowed. 'Does that include the Communists?'

Falk didn't hesitate. 'Absolutely. They hate the Nazis more than anyone.'

Huber's frown deepened. 'I don't doubt their distaste for the Nazi Party,' he said carefully, 'but I want nothing to do with them.'

A brief, uncomfortable silence followed.

Hans was quick to step in. He refused to let the meeting turn sour. 'I don't have a problem working with Communists,' he said, his voice measured but firm. 'Whatever it takes to defeat National Socialism.'

'Neither do I,' said Alex.

Professor Huber remained silent.

Falk moved on. 'Can you and Alex come to Berlin?' he asked Hans. 'I want you to meet some people there.'

Hans and Alex exchanged glances.

A flicker of understanding and excitement passed between them.

'Absolutely,' Hans said. 'When and where?'

'Kaiser Wilhelm Memorial Church. Kurfürstendamm. Six o'clock. Thursday, 25 February.'

The date was set. Hans and Alex were going to Berlin.

Chapter
Twenty-Nine

February 1943

'Traitors! Scum! You have betrayed your country! Betrayed your fellow Germans! You are worse than the foreign enemy!'

Judge Roland Freisler bellows, his voice reverberating off the wood-panelled walls. His face is flushed red with fury, veins bulging in his neck. He flings his arms wildly, his robes billowing like those of some grotesque executioner.

No one dares to intervene. The other judges sit silently on the bench.

My defence lawyer looks as if he might faint. Pale, sweating, he shrinks back in his chair, eyes darting between me and Freisler. It is painfully obvious that he will not speak for me. He cannot. He is too afraid.

Freisler slams his palm down on the bench.

'Bring in the evidence!'

Doors open. Officials file in, arms laden with the remnants of our work. Stacks of leaflets. The duplicating machine. The tins of paint and the stencils used for graffiti.

The spectators gasp.

My stomach twists.

They must have torn through our apartment. They must have ransacked Eickemeyer's studio, turning over every drawer, pulling up every floorboard, searching for anything that could condemn us further.

Hans stares ahead, expression blank, but I know him well enough to recognise the rage simmering beneath the surface. Christoph, beside me, looks down, his hands clenched into fists.

It breaks my heart to see all our efforts – the leaflets, the words we fought so hard to put into the world – reduced to evidence of our so-called treason.

The prosecution calls its witnesses.

First, Jakob Schmidt, the university caretaker who caught us in the act. Then Robert Mohr, the Gestapo officer who interrogated me, and Anton Mahler, who questioned Hans.

Schmidt takes the stand, his chest puffed out, practically preening in front of the audience. He looks immensely pleased with himself, relishing his moment of importance.

'I always knew there was something suspicious about those two,' he declares, nodding toward Hans and me. His tone is smug, self-satisfied.

A lie.

He had never noticed us before that day in the Lichthof, had never given us a second glance. But I imagine he has recounted this story many times, each retelling more exaggerated than the last, until even he has begun to believe his own embellishments.

Mohr and Mahler give their testaments. Their accounts are clinical, devoid of emotion. They describe how we denied everything – until the evidence was stacked too high to refute. How we tried to take all the blame on ourselves.

But Mohr does not mention how he tried to persuade me to save myself. How he gave me a way out, and I refused it. He knows that Freisler will not tolerate any mention of mercy.

Freisler, pleased with what he has heard, nods in satisfaction. He has been given exactly what he wanted – a full confirmation of our guilt.

There are no witnesses for the defence.

Freisler leans forward, his bony finger stabbing the air. 'How could any German do what you have done?'

I jump to my feet before he can continue.

'Somebody had to do something!' I shout, my voice sharp, clear, unwavering. 'We said and wrote what thousands of Germans believe. They just don't have the courage to say it out loud!'

A gasp ripples through the courtroom. I don't know if they are shocked by my outburst or by the implication that there are many more like us out there. That resistance is not limited to the *White Rose*.

Freisler's face contorts with rage. 'Each prisoner may make a final statement,' he snarls, barely controlling his fury.

I shake my head. I have said my piece. Hans remains silent. But Christoph rises to his feet.

His voice is steady, measured. The voice of a man who refuses to cower. 'I did what I did because I love my country,' he says. 'I wanted to see an end to the bloodshed. I didn't want another Stalingrad.'

Angry murmurs ripple through the room. A few men in the crowd shout in outrage.

Christoph does not flinch. 'I ask for clemency – for the sake of my wife, who is ill, and for my three young children.'

Silence.

For the first time, Freisler does not shout. I hold my breath, watching him, waiting. But I see no mercy in his narrow, pitiless eyes.

Then Hans speaks up, his voice urgent. 'Christoph had virtually nothing to do with the *White Rose*. He deserves leniency!'

Freisler whirls on him. 'If you have nothing to say for yourself, then keep your mouth shut!'

Hans slumps back into his seat, defeated.

There's a disturbance at the entrance. The heavy wooden doors bang open. All heads turn.

Freisler's eyes narrow. 'What is going on?'

A voice shouts – one that sends my heart leaping.

'Let me through!'

I know that voice. My pulse quickens. For the first time since this nightmare began, hope flares within me.

Chapter Thirty

January 1943

'We can't print this!' Hans tossed Professor Huber's leaflet onto the table, his face tense.

It was only after Falk Harnack and Professor Huber left that Hans had a chance to read through the whole text.

Alex picked it up and scanned it. The room fell silent except for the soft rustle of paper as his eyes darted across the lines.

After a moment, Alex exhaled sharply. 'Bloody hell.' He slapped the leaflet down. 'There's no way we're printing that bit. But the rest of it is brilliant.'

'I agree,' Hans said.

I crossed my arms. 'What does it say?'

Alex handed me the pages and tapped a particular paragraph. 'That.'

I took my time reading, letting the weight of Huber's words settle over me.

The leaflet opened with a scathing sarcasm, thanking Hitler for the deaths of 330,000 German men. Then came the defiance:

> *Do we wish to sacrifice the rest of German youth for the*
> *base ambitions of a Party clique? No, never! The day of*
> *reckoning has come!*

Yes. This was exactly the kind of language we needed. The fire, the urgency. I read on.

Huber decried the loss of personal freedom, calling it *'our most precious treasure.'* He exposed the lies of the regime, the rotting foundation of the Nazi state. He tore into the SA, the SS, and the Hitler Youth, accusing them of being:

> *Godless, arrogant, and conscienceless exploiters and ex-*
> *ecutioners – blind, stupid adherents of the Führer.*

And then I found the part that had stopped Hans cold.

> *Students must support our glorious Wehrmacht.*

My stomach sank. No wonder Hans and Alex wouldn't stand for it. The Wehrmacht glorious?

Hans was already pacing when he said, 'We need to talk to him.'

That was how, a day later, Professor Huber found himself in our apartment, sitting stiffly across from Hans and Alex while I hovered nearby.

The mood was strained from the outset. Alex, never one for subtlety, didn't waste time.

'This part has to go.' He tapped the offending words. '*Glorious Wehrmacht?* We can't print that.'

Professor Huber's head trembled – a telltale sign of his growing agitation.

'Wh – what do you mean?' he stammered.

Alex leaned forward, his voice sharp. 'I mean that we cannot endorse the Wehrmacht in any way. The army is a pillar of the Nazi state.'

Huber's face reddened. His trembling hand gripped the edge of the table.

'You are wrong,' he said. His voice wavered, but his conviction did not. 'The Wehrmacht is not the Party. It is Germany's army.'

'An army that has enabled Hitler's madness,' Hans countered.

Huber's eyes flashed. 'Do you not understand? If we turn against the Wehrmacht, we turn against the very men who could one day overthrow Hitler!'

Alex's jaw tightened. 'We are fighting for Germany's soul, not its militarism. If we include this, people will think we're just another nationalist faction.'

Huber's breathing grew shallow. 'Then give me back my leaflet.' His hand trembled as he reached for the pages. 'Either you print all of it, or none of it.'

A tense silence filled the room.

Hans's voice was quiet, but unmovable. 'No.'

'Is that your final decision?' asked Huber.

'It is,' said Hans.

'Then I want nothing more to do with you.' Professor Huber picked up his hat and stormed out of the apartment.

I wanted to run after him and apologise, but Hans stopped me. 'Let him go,' he said. 'We have what we need.'

Still, I felt bad for dear Professor Huber. None of us saw him again after that day.

By mid-February, Fritz was finally safe from the frontline and well enough to write me a long letter.

He had imagined being transported in a mobile surgical train, the kind he'd seen in magazines and newsreels – clean white sheets, efficient nurses, quiet dignity.

Instead, the reality was brutal.

The wounded were herded into a cattle car, packed so tightly there was no room to lie down. They had to tend to their own wounds, to each other, as the train crawled along for six endless days. Rain leaked through the roof, soaking their bandages, their uniforms, their bones.

At last, they reached the field hospital in Lemberg, Ukraine. The next day, two of Fritz's fingers were amputated. It was his twenty-sixth birthday.

But what troubled Fritz more than the physical pain, more than the frustration of missing fingers, was the isolation.

His roommate was a stereotypical career officer – arrogant, rigid, convinced of his own importance. They argued about everything until the officer requested a transfer, choosing instead to share a room with an SS lieutenant.

> *More than anything, I want to return to Germany. But it seems the wounded from Stalingrad are being kept away. They must be afraid of what we will say.*

I wrote back immediately.

> *Every day, I run to the post-box, hoping that if I check myself, I'll find a letter waiting. Until now, my hopes have been dashed. It must be so difficult for you to write with your injured hand!*

There were rumours that next term, female students would be sent to work in munitions factories instead of continuing their studies. I wasn't as unhappy about it as I might have been. I explained to Fritz:

> *It's easier to feel compassion for others when you're suffering yourself.*

More than anything, I just wanted to see him again.

> *'I have so much to tell you. When will you come?'*

Two days later, I wrote again.

> *Yesterday, I bought a beautiful blooming stalk. It sits on my desk, bathed in sunlight from the window. Its delicate purple flowers bring joy to my eyes, to my heart. I wish you could see it before it fades. When will you come?*

With Fritz out of the war, recovering in a hospital bed, I felt a door had closed on one part of my life. But another part had just begun. I wrote:

Perhaps we can begin again, someplace new.

By now, the Gestapo must have been in possession of dozens, hundreds, possibly thousands of our leaflets. Overzealous citizens – afraid of the consequences of being caught with subversive literature – would have hurried to hand them in. We had no doubt that the Gestapo were hunting for the authors. They were also scouring Munich for the graffiti artists who had defaced public buildings with their slogans.

At the university, they prowled the halls, their sharp eyes scanning every face. A bulletin circulated, offering a reward for anyone with information about the so-called smear campaign. They probably assumed the graffiti was a reaction to Gauleiter Giesler's speech – which, in truth, it was. But whether they had connected the slogans to the leaflets was another matter entirely.

There was no way to find out without incriminating ourselves, so we asked no questions. We watched and listened in silence.

For a short while, I returned to Ulm to help Mother and Inge, who were both unwell. I took over the household chores, wringing out laundry by hand until my fingers ached and trembled.

I also wrote letters to Fritz, though I received none in return. Every day, I ran to the post-box, hoping – but each day, my hopes were dashed.

The weather was fickle, shifting from snow to sudden sunshine. It matched my mood, which was as restless as the wind. I had vivid, colourful dreams of the future, yet I knew I would likely be drafted for war work next semester.

In the middle of February, I boarded the train back to Munich, knowing the shift it would bring. That journey always transformed me – from an exuberant child into a self-contained adult. Isn't it strange how a few miles can change a person?

By then, production of the sixth leaflet was underway – without Professor Huber's blessing. The text had been finalised and typed, with the contentious phrase about the Wehrmacht removed. We prepared the stencils and, once again, worked through the night, our hands cranking the duplicating machine, our nerves stretched to breaking point.

Hans was determined to distribute this leaflet at the university. He felt – rightly, I believe – that Professor Huber had written it for students.

But while Hans's commitment deepened, Christoph's doubts grew.

'The Nazis are becoming more unstable,' Christoph warned. 'As they lose their grip on the war, they'll execute people just for saying the wrong thing.'

Hans waved him off. 'Don't worry. I'm always careful.'

But Christoph wasn't convinced. And neither was I. There was something feverish about Hans these days – something that frightened me. He moved as if possessed, driven by an energy he couldn't contain.

We were all under too much pressure, surviving on too little sleep, with fear gnawing at our nerves. The bombing raids didn't help – but they weren't the root cause of our exhaustion. It was the constant strain of secrecy, of knowing every moment could be the last.

I felt it, too. My head ached constantly, my thoughts scattered. If only there were an end in sight.

I sought refuge in music.

When we had finished printing the leaflets, I returned to my room, placed a record on the phonograph, and let Schubert's Trout Quintet wash over me.

Oh, how I loved this music.

I closed my eyes, surrendering to the exquisite melodies. The fourth movement, the andantino, never failed to lift my spirits. It always made me laugh, made me want to be a trout myself, darting through clear waters, carefree and full of life.

I imagined springtime clouds, branches trembling with blossoms, the first warmth of the sun after winter's grip.

When I listened to this music, I felt it – the sheer joy of being alive.

That night, I wrote a letter to my friend Lisa Remppis. And then, I fell asleep with Schubert's music still swimming through my mind.

The next day, Hans and I would take the leaflets to the university.

They were already packed in a suitcase.

Chapter Thirty-One

February 1943

My heart leaps as I see Father – my hero – pushing past the guards, forcing his way into the courtroom. Mother is right behind him, clutching at his arm, her face drained of colour. And then I see Werner, my younger brother, still in uniform, on leave from the front. My breath catches. They must have taken the first available train to Munich, desperate to reach us in time.

Mother looks on the verge of collapse, her eyes wide with anguish as she catches sight of me. The pain in her face pierces my heart. I want to run to her, to throw my arms around her, to reassure her – but the guards at my sides clamp down on my shoulders, ensuring I remain seated.

Father does not falter. In a room thick with black and brown uniforms, he stands tall, unafraid. He marches straight to my so-called defence lawyer, who visibly shrinks from his approach.

Father speaks in low, forceful tones, his finger stabbing toward the bench. Even though I can't hear his words, I know what he's saying. He is demanding justice.

A murmur ripples through the packed courtroom. The spectators crane their necks, whispering among themselves, their gazes darting between Father's defiant stance and the judge's scowling face.

The lawyer hesitates, then, reluctantly, makes his way toward Freisler's bench.

Freisler's pallid skin flushes deep red beneath the harsh courtroom lights, matching the scarlet robes that engulf him. And then he explodes.

'Get that man out of my court!' he bellows, his voice splitting the air like a gunshot.

The guards descend. I flinch as they seize Father, wrenching him backward, as if trying to rip him away from me, from this moment, from history itself. Mother cries out. Werner clenches his fists, his body taut with rage, but there is nothing he can do. The guards drag them toward the door.

But Father resists – twisting, fighting against their grip, his voice rising above the din. 'There is a higher justice!'

The courtroom erupts, gasps and murmurs clashing with the thunder of Freisler's fist slamming down on his desk.

The guards shove Father through the doors, but just before he disappears, his final words ring out, fierce and unwavering: 'They will go down in history!'

A moment of pure, ringing silence follows.

Chapter Thirty-Two

February 1943

F reisler makes a great spectacle of himself, scooping up his papers with a flourish and sweeping out of the courtroom as if he were an actor on stage. His scarlet robes billow behind him. The other judges scurry after him, their black robes fluttering in his wake, a murder of crows following their leader. They are going to 'consider' their verdict.

As if there is anything to consider.

A low hum of anticipation spreads through the courtroom. Chatter swells, punctuated by yawns and stretches. For the spectators, this morning's trial has turned out to be far more thrilling than they expected – a bit of drama in their otherwise routine service to the Reich.

Father's outburst has shocked them.

Some mutter in incredulous outrage, shaking their heads. Others glance over their shoulders uneasily, as if fearing association with his defiance.

Deep down, I fear for him. I pray he won't be arrested for interrupting the People's Court.

The spectators drift toward the doors, seeking coffee, cigarettes, fresh air – anything to break the tension. The guards don't move. Hans, Christoph, and I remain seated, watched like caged animals.

Time slows. A strange, unnatural stillness settles over me. I stare at the empty judge's bench and think of all the things that will never happen now.

I will never finish my studies.

I will never marry.

Hans will never go to Berlin to meet Falk Harnack. Three days from now, Falk will wait for him, standing by the Kaiser Wilhelm Memorial Church on the Kurfürstendamm, glancing at his watch, scanning the crowd. What will he do when Hans doesn't show? Will he think we lost courage?

Remorse blooms in my chest. We should have left the university when we had the chance. We should never have gone up to the top floor.

And I should never have pushed those leaflets off the balustrade, never drawn Jakob Schmidt's attention.

That moment – the flutter of paper against the still, heavy air of the Lichthof – sealed our fate. I brought this on myself, on Hans, on Christoph, on our parents. On Fritz. I could weep with regret.

But then, a thought steadies me.

If I could wind back the clock, if I could live my life again, would I still choose the *White Rose?* Would I still fight?

The answer rises in me, unshakable, unyielding.

Yes.

Even knowing it would lead me here, to this courtroom, to this moment of no return.

Yes.

After an hour or so – just long enough for everyone except us to have eaten their lunch and refreshed themselves – the spectators surge back into the courtroom. They don't want to miss the final act of today's theatrical spectacle.

I scan the crowd, searching for familiar faces. No sign of Father, Mother, or Werner. They've been denied entry to the courtroom. I fear what will happen to them now.

Freisler sweeps back onto the bench, his scarlet robes swirling around him. His black-robed judges shuffle in behind him, their expressions impassive, their verdict already written.

The room falls silent.

'The defendants will stand!'

I rise slowly, as if in a dream. Maybe it's the lack of food and water, or maybe some deeper instinct trying to shield me, but I feel detached from reality. As if this is happening to somebody else. Not me. Not Sophie Scholl, twenty-one years old, fourth child of Robert and Magdalena Scholl.

Freisler's voice booms out, dragging me back to the present.

'For the protection of the German people and of the Reich, in this time of mortal struggle, the Court has only one just verdict open to it on the basis of the evidence: the death penalty. With this sentence, the People's Court demonstrates its solidarity with the fighting troops!'

The death penalty.

The words slice through me, but I don't react. I knew this was coming. And yet – to hear it spoken aloud.

Hans suddenly finds his voice. 'You will soon stand where we are now!' he shouts, his voice ringing out like a prophecy.

But Freisler doesn't react. He doesn't flinch, doesn't acknowledge the truth in Hans's words. He's already exiting the room, his robes trailing behind him, his task for the day done.

The guards waste no time. They grab our arms, clamp handcuffs around our wrists, and march us from the courtroom. As we pass through the crush of bodies, the spectators jostle forward, eager for one last glimpse of the students who dared to challenge the Reich.

In the corridor, Werner pushes forward through the crowd, his face pale, eyes wide, brimming with tears. Before the guards can stop him, he clasps our handcuffed hands in turn.

His lips part as if to speak but no words come. There is nothing to say. He already knows.

Hans grasps his hand. 'Stay strong. No compromises.'

Werner nods sharply.

And then the guards shove him aside. The moment is over. They march us on.

Chapter Thirty-Three

February 1943

S tadelheim.

The name alone carries a finality that settles heavy on my chest. This is where they have brought us. A vast, imposing prison complex in the south of the city.

Are these cold, grey walls going to be the last place I see? In a world bursting with beauty, will my final sight be concrete and iron bars?

I close my eyes for a moment and imagine spring meadows, wild with colour. A river, bright and fast, tugging at my feet as I wade in. The scent of pine after rain.

I want to run, to feel the earth beneath me.

But here I am.

The prison staff are not Gestapo. They are ordinary civilians, just men and women doing their jobs, and I sense their unease. I catch them watching us with puzzled expressions – three young students, so small and unthreatening, condemned to die as enemies of the state.

They process us, reducing us to numbers.

Christoph is 524.

Hans is 525.

I am 526. The last trace of my identity stripped away.

Hans and Christoph have to change into striped cotton prison uniforms, but I am allowed to keep my clothes. Perhaps they don't have a uniform that fits me. Perhaps it doesn't matter. They don't expect me to be here long enough to need one.

There's a quiet discussion among the guards. A decision is made, and then the guard in charge walks toward us.

'Your parents are here,' he says. 'They want to see you.'

I'm overjoyed they are here and relieved they have not been taken into custody.

'Normally it wouldn't be allowed,' he continues, 'but... under the circumstances...' He trails off.

Under the circumstances. The words hang between us, unspoken yet deafening.

Hans goes first. He walks tall, his head high. He wanted our parents to be proud of him, and they will be.

I feel a pang of sorrow for Christoph. He has no one here. His wife doesn't even know that, soon, she will be a widow. That her three young children will grow up without a father.

And then it's my turn. A woman prison guard leads me down a corridor. We enter a small meeting room. Mother and Father stand on the other side of a waist-high barrier. They look tired, worn, their faces etched with grief. But they stand strong for my sake.

We clasp hands. For a moment, no one speaks. There is so much to say. And so little time to say it. Where do you even begin?

Mother's voice is barely above a whisper. 'We only heard on Friday you'd been arrested.' Today is Monday. We were arrested Thursday. 'Traute Lafrenz and Otl Aicher came to see us. We wanted to come straight away, but... they don't allow visitors in Gestapo headquarters over the weekend.' Her words tumble out in a rush. 'We left first thing this morning and got here as soon as we could.'

I squeeze her hands. 'I'm so glad you came.'

'A young law student introduced himself to us at the courthouse,' says Father. 'Leo Samberger. Do you know him?'

I shake my head.

Father continues. 'He sat through the whole trial. As soon as the verdict was announced, he ran outside to tell us. He said we should go straight to the prosecutor's office and file a plea for clemency, which we've done.'

I know their actions will be futile, but I smile at him anyway. 'Thank you.'

But it's comforting, knowing that in that crowd of jeering faces, there was at least one person on our side.

Mother's grip tightens around my fingers. Her face is pale, stricken. 'Oh, Sophie. To think you'll never walk through the door again.' Her voice breaks, her eyes shining with unshed tears.

I want to comfort her, to somehow ease the unbearable weight of grief pressing down on her.

'Mother,' I say gently, 'what are a few years, compared to eternity?'

A soft sob escapes her lips.

Father looks at me, his gaze steady, unwavering. 'What you did, Sophie, it was right. We are proud of you.'

His words fill me with warmth. I needed to hear that.

'We took everything upon ourselves,' I say, my voice firm. 'What we did will make waves.'

Mother's hands tighten around mine. 'Remember Jesus.' Tears slip down her cheeks.

I nod. 'You too.'

I smile at them as the guard touches my arm. Time's up. They remain standing as I'm led away.

Their faces stay with me. Always.

Chapter Thirty-Four

February 1943

T he light in my cell has dimmed. The air has a stillness about it, as if the world is holding its breath.

A key turns in the lock. The door opens, and the prison chaplain steps inside. He looks nervous. I wonder if he has ever had to prepare someone so young for death before.

'I've just seen your brother,' he says softly.

'How is he?'

'Calm. He wanted to read Psalm 90.'

'That sounds like a good idea.'

The chaplain opens his Bible, and together we read the words:

> *Lord, you have been our dwelling-place throughout all generations. Before the mountains were born or you brought forth the earth and the world, from everlasting to everlasting you are God.*

A quiet peace settles over me. Then we turn to another passage, one I have always loved. Corinthians, Chapter 13.

If I speak in the tongues of men and of angels, but have not love, I am only a resounding gong or a clanging cymbal... And now these three remain: faith, hope, and love. But the greatest of these is love.

The chaplain's voice trembles as he reads from John's Gospel:

Greater love has no man than this, that he lay down his life for his friends.

He closes his Bible and looks at me with eyes full of sorrow. 'This is what you, your brother, and your friend have done.'

I do not need to reply. He sees it in my face. I am at peace.

'God bless you, my child.'

It is almost time.

Footsteps echo in the corridor outside. Keys rattle in the lock. The guards enter and take me to a small, bare room where Hans and Christoph are waiting. For a moment, we just look at one another. No words are needed.

A guard hesitates, then reaches into his pocket. 'Here,' he says, offering us a single cigarette.

It's an unexpected gesture, perhaps even a risky one. He's probably breaking a dozen different rules.

Hans nods in thanks. The guard strikes a match and lights the cigarette.

Then we are left alone.

Hans inhales deeply before passing it to me. I don't usually smoke. But tonight, I do. I breathe in slowly, feeling the warmth in my lungs. Then I pass it to Christoph. We share a cigarette, the three of us. A simple, human act, in the face of the inhuman.

Christoph exhales a stream of smoke and gives a small, wistful smile. 'I didn't know dying would be so easy,' he says. He looks at me, then at Hans. 'In just a few minutes, we'll see each other again in Heaven.'

The guard returns.

It's time.

'Fräulein Scholl.'

I take a breath. Steady. Strong. I turn to Hans and Christoph. 'Goodbye.'

'See you soon,' Christoph whispers.

Hans reaches for my hand, his grip firm, unwavering. No fear.

The guards step forward, manacle my wrists, and lead me away.

The cold air hits me like a wave as they lead me across the courtyard. I look up. The sky is a cloudless blue. I drink in the sight, memorising it. The crispness of the air. The whisper of the wind against my skin. I inhale deeply, holding the moment in my lungs.

Then I step inside a small, silent building. There is only one object in the room. The guillotine stands in the centre. The blade gleams silver.

One of the guards speaks. 'Kneel down.'

I do as they ask. No fear. I place my head on the block.

'Sweet Jesus,' I pray.

And then–

Silence.

Epilogue

On Monday, 22 February 1943, at five o'clock in the evening, Sophie Scholl was executed by guillotine. She was twenty-one years old.

A few minutes later, Christoph Probst followed. He was twenty-three, a husband, a father of three small children.

Finally, Hans Scholl was led across the courtyard. He carried himself with the same defiant courage he had shown in the courtroom. Just before entering the execution chamber, he called out in a loud, clear voice: 'Long live freedom!'

Then the blade fell.

Robert and Magdalena Scholl left Munich on Monday, hoping – against the odds – that their appeal process would succeed.

The next day, their worst fears were confirmed. The executions were publicly announced in Munich.

The Gestapo moved swiftly. The entire Scholl family was arrested. Only Werner, still on leave from the Eastern Front, was spared.

Inge, Elisabeth, and Magdalena were held until July 1943. Robert Scholl was sentenced to two years in prison for raising children who had dared to defy the Reich.

Willi Graf was also arrested on the evening of Thursday 18 February 1943 but, for reasons known only to the Gestapo, not put on trial with Sophie, Christoph and Hans. He would be tried later.

Meanwhile, Alex Schmorell was on the run.

With the help of his friend Lilo Ramdohr, he obtained false papers and fled to Innsbruck. He planned to hide in a camp for foreign workers under a false identity. But his Ukrainian contact never showed up. Forced to keep moving, he sought refuge in the mountains, aided by Russian friends. But a local betrayed him. Desperate, he fled deeper into the mountains, but snowstorms and exhaustion forced him to turn back.

He returned to Munich, hoping to find help from a former girlfriend, Marie Luise. On the night of 24 February, during an RAF bombing raid, Alex appeared in the basement of her apartment block, seeking shelter. He was weak, starving, and dishevelled. The women in the shelter panicked. Alex's face was plastered across the city on wanted posters. The Gestapo had put a 1,000-Mark reward on his head. Marie Luise hesitated. Her friends urged her to turn him in. Alex knew the game was up. A call was placed. The moment the all-clear siren sounded, a black Gestapo car arrived. Alex Schmorell was taken to the Wittelsbach Palace.

Others were arrested in quick succession: Traute Lafrenz, Gisela Schertling, Hans and Susanne Hirzel from Ulm, Herr Grimminger from Stuttgart, Falk Harnack, and others only marginally involved. And Professor Kurt Huber, the author of the sixth and final leaflet.

Professor Huber had witnessed Hans and Sophie's arrest in the Lichthof. He must have realised immediately that they had been caught distributing his leaflet. He went home and burned his papers.

Two days later, early in the morning, while his wife was away bartering for food, the Gestapo arrived at his house. His twelve-year-old daughter, Birgit, answered the door.

They pushed past her and took her father away. Professor Huber was not just arrested. He was stripped of his professorship, leaving his family with nothing. Alone in his cell, he continued working on his unfinished book on Leibniz, determined to leave something for his wife and children.

On Monday 19 April 1943, the second trial of the *White Rose* took place.

This time, Alex Schmorell, Willi Graf, and Professor Huber stood before Roland Freisler. There was no pretence of justice. They were all convicted of high treason and sentenced to death.

Other members – like Traute Lafrenz – received prison sentences of varying lengths.

On 13 July 1943, Alex Schmorell and Professor Kurt Huber were guillotined.

Willi Graf remained in Gestapo custody. They kept him alive, hoping he would reveal more names. He never did. On 12 October 1943, after months of interrogation, he too was executed.

After Sophie was arrested, her mother, Magdalena Scholl, wrote to Fritz Hartnagel, by then in Poland.

He rushed back to Germany, calling from Berlin, only to be told by Werner that Sophie and Hans were already dead. The rest of the Scholl family was in prison.

Fritz survived the war. He married Sophie's sister, Liesl, with whom he had four children. He became a judge and spent the rest of his life campaigning against German rearmament.

Magdalena Scholl did not live long after the war. Robert Scholl became mayor of Ulm under American occupation. Werner Scholl was declared missing in action on the Eastern Front. He never returned.

Inge Scholl married Otl Aicher and dedicated her life to keeping the memory of the *White Rose* alive. She founded a school, built on humanist ideals.

And what of the leaflets?

The Gestapo could not erase their words. Despite their efforts to silence the White Rose, their leaflets continued to spread. Copies were smuggled throughout Germany and occupied Europe. They reached neutral Sweden and Switzerland. From there, they found their way to London.

The Allies reprinted thousands of copies. The RAF dropped them over German cities. Clara Huber, the widow of Professor Huber, was summoned to Gestapo headquarters. Clara knew nothing.

But she left the interrogation room with her head held high. She had just learned that the words of her husband – and the *White Rose* – had reached an audience beyond anything they could have dreamed.

The White Rose had not been silenced.

Their words lived on.

Select
Bibliography

Hans Scholl / Sophie Scholl, *At the Heart of the White Rose: Letters and Diaries of Hans and Sophie Scholl* (edited by Inge Jens, translated by J. Maxwell Brownjohn, preface by Richard Gilman)

Annette Dumbach and Jud Newborn, *Sophie Scholl and the White Rose*

Richard Hanser, *A Noble Treason: The story of Sophie Scholl & the White Rose Revolt against Hitler*

Hermann Vinke, *Das kurze Leben der Sophie Scholl*

Inge Scholl, *The White Rose: Munich 1942-1943* (translated by Arthur R. Schulze)

Rupert Colley, *Nazi Germany*

Maren Gottschalk, *Schluss. Jetzt werde ich etwas tun: Die Lebensgeschichte der Sophie Scholl*

Sophie Scholl / Fritz Hartnagel, *Damit wir uns nicht verlieren: Briefwechsel 1937-1943* (herausgegeben von Thomas Hartnagel)

Ruth Hanna Sachs, *White Rose History: Volume 1 – Coming Together*

Ruth Hannah Sachs, *White Rose History: Volume 2 – Journey to Freedom*

About the author

OTHER BOOKS BY MARGARITA MORRIS

Oranges for Christmas
Goodbye to Budapest
A Long Way From Warsaw

ABOUT THE AUTHOR

Shortlisted for the Amazon Breakthrough Novel Award in 2014 with her first novel, *Oranges for Christmas*, Margarita brings a love of history to her writing. She studied languages at Oxford and it was as a student that she visited Berlin and saw at first hand the effects of the Berlin Wall on this divided city. Years later this experience led her to write *Oranges for Christmas* about a family trying to escape from Communist East Berlin. Since then she has written about the 1956 Hungarian Uprising in *Goodbye to Budapest* and the experience of Poland in World War II in *A Long Way From Warsaw*. She lives in Oxfordshire with her husband Steve. Together they write crime fiction under the pen name, M S Morris.

www.ingramcontent.com/pod-product-compliance
Lightning Source LLC
Chambersburg PA
CBHW030329200626
46816CB00006BA/1984